Kit looked up to smile at the man, then caught her breath in a soundless gasp as he swung round to face her. Her first thought was . . . it can't be true . . . it can't, it can't be him . . . it can't be the same man, not possibly, yet she knew, she just knew it was! She had not known his name when they'd met at a wedding nearly three years ago; they had met, and clashed, and exchanged heated words, following an incident that had very nearly led to tragedy . . .

Whether he remembered her or not, she was unable to tell; his face with its craggy, uneven features showed little expression at all. She, however, remembered him with an accuracy that startled her . . . the thick fair hair, the deep blue eyes, the long straight nose, sprang at her, out of the past, in a flare of recognition. Charles Niall wasn't a man one could forget.

Janet Ferguson was born at Newmarket, Suffolk. She nursed as a V.A.D. during the Second World War, then became a medical secretary working in hospitals in London and the provinces and (more latterly) in Brighton, Sussex, where she now lives. She has had nineteen novels published—eight of them being Doctor Nurse Romances. These, she says, she finds the most satisfying and interesting to plot: 'I couldn't be happy unless I had a story to weave. My characters are nearly as real to me as my friends and colleagues, several of whom are nurses and who—sometimes unwittingly—supply me with the kind of material I can use.'

Janet Ferguson's recent titles include *Sister on Penhallow Ward*, *Nurse on Livingstone Ward* and *Surgeon on Call*.

THE HOSPITAL SUMMER

BY

JANET FERGUSON

MILLS & BOON LIMITED
ETON HOUSE 18–24 PARADISE ROAD
RICHMOND SURREY TW9 1SR

First published in Great Britain 1988
by Mills & Boon Limited

ISBN 0 263 76043 X

Set in 10 on 11 pt Linotron Times
03–0488–55,490

Photoset by Rowland Phototypesetting Limited
Bury St Edmunds, Suffolk
Made and printed in Great Britain by
William Collins Sons & Co. Limited, Glasgow

CHAPTER ONE

BEWLIS General Hospital was a town within a town. The rise of ground on which it stood gave its sprawling buildings and blocks a fine view of the Downs on two sides, while from its south-facing windows the glimmering line of the English Channel could be glimpsed on a clear sunny day. 'It's a healthy spot,' people would say, 'it's a good spot for a hospital.' They had been saying that now for a very long time, for nearly a hundred years when the first of the buildings went up on Castle Hill.

The town had an historical elegance, it was packed with tourists in summer. It was spring now, the beginning of May, and it was unseasonably warm. Up at the hospital on the hill the bed-fast patients were puffing and blowing and sighing wearily, complaining about the heat. So was Kit Tennant—Staff Nurse Tennant—who was preparing a dressing trolley in the clinical room off Bellingham Ward, which was women's surgical. Even her light-as-air starched white cap seemed to weigh on her copper-gold hair. Her head felt tight, her skin moist; she loosened the belt of her dress. She wished, if it were going to storm, it would hurry up and do so; she reached for forceps and a stitch-cutter from the shelf.

It was Monday, the main operating day, which meant no visiting. It was three-thirty and nearly teatime, but Kit wasn't hurrying. Her delaying tactics were not due to the heat, but more to do with the fact that Charles Niall, the registrar, was at present in the ward. This was only her second day at the General, but at twenty-five, with close on six years of hospital nursing behind her, she knew most of what there was to know about ethics and protocol, and the do's and don'ts relating to doctors' rounds.

She wondered what Mr Niall was like. She had not even glimpsed him as yet, only heard his footsteps thudding by some ten minutes ago. She had met the houseman, Dick Parker, yesterday—a young, dark-moustached man with a lopsided grin, he had made her feel at home. On the whole she was finding most of the staff to be friendly and welcoming. Sister Clive herself had made a point of saying how glad she was to have another experienced nurse on the ward.

The soft thudding to of the ward doors seemed to indicate some sort of movement. This was followed by a mumble of voices from the direction of Sister's office. That must mean they were out, thought Kit, and safely closeted. Now was her chance . . . she eased the trolley out of the clinical room and began to push it down the corridor.

Everywhere seemed very quiet with no milling visitors, but as she drew level with Sister's office a man backed out of it so suddenly that he very nearly crashed right into her. Sister called out a warning just in time, then said in her lilting voice: 'Mr Niall, this is Mrs Tennant, one of my part-time nurses.'

Getting over the shock of the near collision, Kit looked up to smile at the man, then caught her breath in a soundless gasp as he swung round to face her. Her first thought was . . . it can't be true . . . it can't, it can't be him . . . it can't be the same man, not possibly, yet she knew, she just knew it was! She had not known his name when they'd met at a wedding nearly three years ago; they had met, and clashed, and exchanged heated words, following an incident that had very nearly led to tragedy.

'Good afternoon, Mr Niall.' Somehow she recovered her poise. She had to be polite and speak, she had to cover up. This was Charles Niall, FRCS, first assistant and right-hand man to Professor Planner, the consultant head of the General's surgical team. Whether he remembered her or not, she was unable to tell; his face with its craggy, uneven features showed little expression at all. She, however, remembered him with an accuracy that startled her . . . the thick fair hair, the deep blue eyes, the long straight nose, sprang at her, out of the past, in a flare of recognition. Charles Niall wasn't a man one could forget.

'You work part-time only, do you?' he said in a chippy voice, his eye moving over her sterile trolley as though to find fault with it.

'I don't know about *only*, Mr Niall,' Sister put in quickly. 'Our part-time nurses make a valuable contribution to the work of the ward team. As a matter of fact I sometimes wonder what we would do without them.' Sister Clive, as Kit was already discovering, defended her nurses against all comers, regardless of status or rank.

'Good!' Charles Niall jerked at his coat, slid a folder under his arm, then set off for the landing doors at the end of the corridor. Kit and Sister watched him go, Kit's thoughts running amok. He was tall, broad, powerfully built; his wife had been petite—tiny and pretty, like the little girl. Thinking of the child made her catch her breath again, made that other time she had met him move in her mind like a scoring knife. It's over, it's done, it's all in the past, her commonsense voice said; even so, she couldn't relax till she saw his broad back pass through the corridor doors and out to the lifts.

'He's got an accident case to see down in A and E,' said Sister, wondering a little at the blanched look on Staff Nurse Tennant's face. She must surely be used to the snide remarks that occasionally dropped from the lips of senior doctors, especially when they were rushed. She was surprised at Mr Niall, though; in the three months he had been at the General, she had never at any time known him to be less than courteous. Still, no doubt he had his off days. She turned back into her office. Gathering her wits, Kit proceeded into the ward.

Mrs Bentick, who had had a herniotomy ten days ago, watched the removal of her stitches with stoic calm. 'I hardly felt a thing,' she said, as Kit drew the last one through. 'I like to see what's going on, I'm not the squeamish kind. I saw both my babies born, you know, I didn't intend to miss that.'

'Having stitches out is a shade less exciting,' said Kit, smiling back at her. She tidied her up. She had successfully, for the moment, put Charles Niall out of her thoughts. Removing her disposable mask and gloves, she drew the bed curtains aside. Then asking Learner Nurse Holden to take the trolley out to the sluice, she went forward to meet a stretcher that was being wheeled into the ward by the theatre porters; she looked down at its occupant.

Miss Phipps had been the last patient on Charles Niall's list that day. She was a twenty-three-year-old diabetic, who had developed a foot infection through wearing high fashion, far too narrow shoes. On admission she had been pyrexic, and X-ray had revealed that the metatarsal head of her little toe was eroded. Charles Niall had decided to operate, and she had been in the recovery room for the past forty minutes. She was conscious, but drowsy, she tried to speak and failed. 'You're safely back in the ward now, Miss Phipps,' Kit spoke close to her face. 'You have nothing at all to worry about; everything has gone very well.'

'She's on half-hourly observations of blood pressure and pulse,' said Sister, helping Kit settle her into bed. 'The medical side are responsible for checking her blood glucose level. Ring them, please, tell them she's back. Sister Hart on Cann Ward will arrange it. Nurse Geare,' she summoned a second-year nurse and handed her Miss Phipps' charts, 'I'm putting you in charge of this patient's observations, and remember to make quite sure that her foot stays supported and her dressing is dry and intact. And yes, Mrs Gartside, tea is coming, I can hear the trolley now.' She said this over her shoulder to the patient in bed number nine, who had asked about tea three times in the past half-hour.

'She don't understand how I crave for me cuppa.' Mrs Gartside sighed with pleasure as Kit swung her locker flap over the bed and placed on top of it the longed-for cup of tea and slice of cake. 'When I'm home I keep the kettle on the go all day. It don't take a second to brew up then, I've got a solid fuel Aga, you see.'

'They're good, aren't they?' Kit had got one, hers being oil-fired. Tim, her late husband, had had it converted, he had spared no expense to have the kind of home that would run itself.

'I'm glad me trouble don't bar me from drinking.' Mrs Gartside looked sympathetically at Mrs Farley in the bed opposite who had undergone gastrectomy and was being fed by intravenous drip.

Mrs Gartside's 'trouble' was varicosities. The affected veins had been stripped three days ago, and pressure was being maintained by bandaging. A rise in temperature had kept her in bed, but she hoped to be more mobile on Wednesday when her son from Barhampton was due to visit her. 'I hope Mr Niall will let me get up,' she said as she nibbled her cake. 'What he says goes, you know. Have you met him yet, Nurse?'

'Just briefly, yes, a few minutes ago,' Kit edged away from the bed.

'All the nurses fancy him, I expect you'll be the same.'

'I don't think so.' Kit was guarded, mindful of what she said. Patients loved to gossip and any remark, adverse or otherwise, might be passed round the ward, plus embellishments.

'Mind you,' Mrs Gartside added, 'he's got a stern look to him, but when he smiles, everything changes; you feel all funny inside. He twinkles at you, if you know what I mean; you want to give him a hug.'

'I see,' said Kit, and managed to smile, while her thoughts raced back. Tim had had a twinkle in his eye; it was one of the first of many things that had drawn her to him, like a pin to a magnet, as though she had no will. Tim had been outgoing, vital and charming, a confident, quicksilver man. There were times, even now, when she couldn't believe he was dead.

Leaving Rosa and Marylyn, the ward domestics, to hand round the teas, she went to the central desk and rang Sister Hart on Cann Ward, giving her the message about Miss Phipps. For a while after she had made the call she remained at the desk, her eye running down the two lines of beds as she strove to memorise the names of the patients and the type of surgery each had undergone. She was glad she had returned to ward nursing, and the part-time hours worked out by Sister Clive, which included occasional night duty, suited her home arrangements very well. She considered herself very lucky indeed to have landed a job like this, but oh dear, what mischievous fate had decreed that she should re-meet a man who up until a mere half an hour ago she had not even known was connected with medicine, let alone be in East Sussex, in this hospital, in Professor Planner's team.

She had asked Tim who he was, that day three years ago, Tim said: 'Oh, I don't know—a friend of the bride's, I should think. He and his wife were strangers to me, and I'd like to keep it that way.' Kit agreed and, like Tim, she tried to be flip and dismiss the whole thing. But she had never forgotten the scene, nor the man, and the awfulness of it all, the sheer horror of what *might* have happened, had dogged her daytime thoughts and haunted her dreams for a long time afterwards.

To meet Charles Niall here was the limit. The gods must be splitting their sides, she muttered to herself a few minutes later when, in the nurses' cloakroom, she changed her white uniform dress for a patterned skirt and top. The thunder was starting—a hollow rumbling, distant at first, then closer. The storm was coming, she could smell rain, although none was falling yet—at least not on this side of the Downs—the Downs divided the weather. She hoped to get home before the deluge came.

The lift bore her down to the entrance hall, and as she began to cross the stretch of parquet to the sliding glass doors that parted at one's approach, a zigzag of lightning spiked the sky, while the clap of thunder that followed caused homegoing staff who were out in the yard to leap back inside. One of the hurriedly returning crowd was a tall, broad-shouldered man in a light suit, dark-spotted with rain—Charles Niall! Oh no! Kit groaned. Oh no, not him, perhaps he won't see me—but he did, he could hardly avoid it. She was too late to press back to the lifts from which more staff were disgorging. There was another sizzling flash of lightning, and a bang of thunder so loud that it seemed to make the air dance a jig, to tremble the atmosphere. Within this cavorting violence of sound she felt rather than saw Charles Niall standing in front of her. 'Don't attempt to go out in that,' he said, 'it's right over us now.'

She lip-read his words, while a glance through the doors showed a steel curtain of rain scything down on to the tarmac yard, bouncing up from it, making a fast-flowing stream to the exit gates.

'I'm not dressed for shooting the rapids!' She tried a laugh which didn't come off. She wasn't alarmed by the storm so much as unnerved by the man at her side.

'There's a seat behind you, I should grab it,' he said. Kit looked round and saw a space on the padded form that ran the length of the hall to the foot of the stairs. She did as he said, then someone moved up, and he eased himself in beside her . . . she felt with reluctance, as he didn't look over-pleased. 'You and I have met before, have we not . . . before today, I mean.' His words were a statement and not a query, and Kit's heart gave a jump.

'Yes, at a wedding. I was with my husband, it was nearly three years ago.' She tried her best to sound matter-of-fact, but found it difficult.

'A rowdy wedding,' he said in flat tones.

'Yes, I agree, it was.' And she spoke the truth, she had hated that wedding; it hadn't been her scene.

But this wasn't her scene either, sitting side by side with this man, wondering if she should speak again and, if so, what about. He gave her no openings, no encouragement, and the silence between them went on . . . on and on like stretching cord, while the clamour of the storm over their heads all but deafened them. But after a time, as even the fiercest of storms are bound to do, it began to lessen, to rumble and grumble, to drool away to the coast. In another minute or two she could go, getting wet wouldn't hurt her. She began to make tentative shifting movements, just as Charles Niall said:

'Have you and your husband lived here long?' His question, quietly asked, wasn't at all what Kit had expected, and she was hard put to it to answer it. Even now, after all this time, she disliked explaining to strangers that she was a widow, she just hated saying the words.

'We moved when Tim got his job down here, but he died nineteen months ago.' To be brief was best; she tightened her hands in her lap.

'I didn't know that. Was he ill . . . what happened?' Charles Niall turned his face towards her, he was very close, she could feel his breath on her skin.

'He wasn't ill, he had excellent health—he had a car accident four months and one week after we moved down here.'

Charles Niall gave what looked like a nod and faced front again. Within the chatter of the crowd about them and the dying groans of the storm, Kit couldn't be sure if he volunteered any remark at all. What struck her, however, was his air of un-surprise about how Tim had died. This angered her, for she thought she knew why he sat there looking so bland, sat there with a judging face, summing the situation *and Tim* up, entirely erroneously.

'It was a foggy October evening, there was no other car involved. He struck a bollard, it wasn't his fault,' she put in quickly, trying to control the shaking of her voice.

'It must have been an appalling shock.' At least he did say that. He went through the motions of being polite, but that was all it was. Nevertheless, as he had asked about Tim, it seemed to be the right thing to enquire about his wife and child, but she did so with diffidence.

'I hope Mrs Niall and your daughter are well. Do they like living in Sussex?' In the end she was proud of the courteous yet nonchalant way she brought that out.

A second passed, perhaps two or three, or perhaps those seconds were minutes, then he said: 'There is no Mrs Niall, and I certainly don't have a daughter!' He smiled as he spoke, but meeting his eyes, Kit felt a sense of disquiet. She felt she was treading on delicate ground, felt her colour come up.

'I'm sorry, Mr Niall, I'm afraid we assumed . . .'

'We?' His thick brows lowered, like twin thatches, jutting out over his eyes.

'Tim and I thought . . .'

'Ah yes,' his face cleared, 'I see what you mean. Pairs and trios at weddings are often taken for family units.'

'I think they are.' She seized on this, while cursing herself for a fool. But he had seemed so like a family man, so protective towards the child, and towards the woman too—Kit could see her now, white and shaking, clinging to his arm.

'Where do you live, far from here?' Charles Niall asked, after a pause.

'Half a mile away in Mount Cliff Road, but I have my

car on the park.' She leaned forward and looked across his chest, trying to make out what the weather was doing. Could she make a quick dash?

'It's still pouring, but less so.' And now he sounded amused. Perhaps he guessed how anxious she was to detach herself from his side. 'In a hurry, are you?' He slewed round to face her, and she noted that his mouth was the deep-cut kind with long corners and a straight firm underlip. The corners moved upwards, softening his face, and some rather nice creases rayed out from his eyes, which smiled into hers . . . and instantly she was beguiled, and furious at being so. Again she made movements to go.

'I have to get home, Mr Niall. I think I'll risk it now.' She got up, so did he; he walked with her to the doors. As they neared them the glass parted company, letting in the rain on a sail of wind that drenched Kit's skirt and blew her hair up in the air.

'Some people,' Charles Niall said goodhumouredly, 'actually *like* getting wet!' He watched Kit preparing to leap through the doors as though her feet were on springs. She had the kind of legs usually dubbed 'endless'. She can probably run like a fawn, passed through his mind, while his glance moved up to rest on her face again—pinkly flushed, with freckles across the nose.

'My daughter will be looking out for me.' Kit's hands were on her head, trying to hold down her jaw-length hair, cut in the shape of a bell. 'Dee is the reason I work part-time,' she said with emphasis, but she smiled as well, preparing herself for flight.

He didn't smile back, just muttered 'good night' as the doors slid to between them, setting her free to streak through the rain, imprisoning him inside. Carl Manders from the Neuro-Wing claimed his attention then. A brief discussion followed, then the two of them walked through to A and E, to look at some X-ray films.

CHAPTER TWO

Kit coasted slowly down the hill, windscreen wipers pulsing, the rain beating so hard on the roof that she felt it must come through. Her stop-and-go conversation with Charles Niall still plumed about in her head. So the little girl Tim had nearly knocked down hadn't been his own. Who had the mother been—his girlfriend, perhaps, or she might have been a relative? Somehow she didn't think the latter, for surely he would have said so. There had been something in his attitude too—just now when they were talking—that had signalled a warning, a warning for her to keep off. Goodness knows I was only too willing to drop *that* subject, she thought, as she braked at the lights just before the High Street began. The air was much cooler, the storm had done that, and Kit shivered in her damp clothes. Maybe she shouldn't have been petty enough to fling out that remark about part-time working, just as a parting shot. Her mother would have called it the height of bad taste, she grimaced into her mirror. But it was true what she had told Charles Niall, her eleven-month-old daughter was the reason why she didn't work full-time.

If it hadn't been for her cousin, Peg Carlton, she couldn't have worked at all—at least not at nursing, for which she had a flair. She needed a job, she needed to work, for Tim had left heavy debts, their home being the heaviest of them all, as there had been no insurance policy to take care of the mortgage when he died.

Kit had been very wary about them taking on such a large house. It was Victorian/Edwardian and four-bedroomed, and stood on its own plot of ground in Mount Cliff Road, the 'best' end of the town. 'It's too much for us, Tim, we can't afford it,' she had protested when he took her to view it.

'Don't be silly, darling, of course we can. With the salary I'm earning now we'll have no trouble getting a mortgage, and we'll need all the space in time. You like it, don't you?' He had turned aggrieved eyes to hers.

She did like it, very much; she loved the big high-ceilinged rooms. She was tired, too, of living in the furnished flat in Park Street. They had been cramped up in it for six weeks, having moved there from Kent when Tim got his job as assistant editor of the *Bewlis Gazette*. Their house in Alvestone, Kent, had been sold, and their furniture was in store. They wanted to settle down into a permanent home.

'This is the house for us,' Tim pressed, and against her better judgment Kit agreed, as she so often had, with most of his suggestions. She hated rows and he hated being opposed.

They had been in the house exactly a month when Tim met his death on the London to Brighton road that misty October night. Five weeks later Kit discovered she was pregnant, and four months after that Peg Carlton and her husband, Bob, and their small son, Joe, came to live in the top part of the house.

It hadn't been simply to help Kit out that the Carltons had moved into Hilldown. Bob was a chartered accountant and the company for whom he worked had gone into liquidation at Michaelmas, which had been a bitter blow. With little to tie them to Newhaven—where they had lived at that time—Bob had decided to set up in business on his own. As luck would have it he heard of a small office to let in Bewlis. It was in the High Street and the rent was steep, but if he and Peg sold their house he could just about manage to meet all costs and employ a secretary. The problem was, where would they live, for he couldn't buy again, so when Kit told them she was going to let the top half of Hilldown House, and asked if they felt it would suit them, he and Peg jumped at the chance. There was loads of room and their little boy would have a garden to play in. Right from the start the arrangement had worked out well.

Peg—big, blonde and healthy, with Dee straddling her hip—was standing in the old-fashioned porch with its overhang like a station, as Kit parked the car and raced across the grass. 'Have you been a good little mouse, then?' She took Dee into her arms, loving the feel and the warmth of her, rejoicing in her weight. Dee squealed and wriggled to be set down—she disliked her mother's damp front. Scudding away on hands and knees in her yellow dungarees, she got as far as the stairs, where she managed to pull herself upright, then fell over backwards, making her scolding noise. Kit watched her, aware of a love so deep and acute that it hurt. When Dee had been born, when Kit first held her, she knew that she would die for her . . . willingly, if it ever came to that. She hadn't been a pretty baby, she wasn't pretty now, but she was 'taking', with her scallop of new-penny hair, with her wicked grin, her blue eyes fringed in spiky lashes . . . Tim's eyes, with a twinkle in them too.

'I'll take her into the kitchen with me while you get out of those wet things,' said Peg, as she tucked her daffodil hair back behind her ears.

'Can I go with Aunt Kit, Mummy?' asked Joe. 'I want to show her my drawing.' He was four and attended play-school; he looked anxiously at his mother. He had been told that he was not to intrude into Kit's part of the house unless he was asked—the two families respected one another's privacy. The big square kitchen was the only room they shared.

'You can show it to her later.' Peg watched Kit go out. To her way of thinking her cousin looked wan. Peg was worried about her. She had not been her old self for ages . . . losing Tim, of course, marked the start of that fragile look, and Kit kept a lot to herself. Still, now that she was back to nursing, working with lots of people, she might meet someone suitable and get married again, to someone older and . . . yes, and *wiser* than Tim had ever been. Tim, Peg considered, had never really grown up.

'So, how have things gone today?' she asked when Kit, in jeans and shirt that made her look more reed-slim than ever, returned to the kitchen and got on her hands and knees with Dee on the floor.

'Oh, all right,' said Kit, but Peg picked up the uncertainty in her voice.

'But?' she prompted.

'Well, something rather *awkward* happened, Peg.'

'Go on, then, you can't leave it there.' Peg turned round from the sink, wiping her hands on a square of kitchen towel.

'I was introduced to the registrar, Charles Niall,' Kit began. 'I discovered that I'd met him before when . . . I didn't know who he was. It was at a wedding reception in Hampstead, nearly three years ago. I was with Tim, it was when we were living in Kent.'

'Interesting! Was he pleased to see you?'

'Quite the reverse, I think. I certainly wasn't pleased to see him.' Kit bit down hard on her lip.

'I scent a mystery. Tell me about it. Whose wedding was it?' Peg watched her cousin perch on a stool.

'The bridegroom's name was Peter Haines. He was a Fleet Street journalist, and Tim had worked with him on the *Alverstone Echo* in Kent, at one time. Anyway, we were asked to the wedding . . . a very big affair. Tim met a lot of old friends there, rather a boisterous lot.'

'Hard-drinking types?'

'Well . . . yes.'

'And Tim went over the top?'

'He wasn't legless, if that's what you mean, but yes, he drank a fair bit,' Kit admitted. 'I was driving home, though, we'd arranged that, talked about it beforehand.

So there was no real reason why he shouldn't enjoy himself. But the thing was he kept the car keys and wouldn't give them up. He was fooling about, acting silly—it was no more than that. When we were leaving the hotel he rushed to the car and got in the driving seat. Even then I didn't really think he meant to start it up. When he switched on and took the brake off, I was in the car like lightning. I tried to stop him, we struggled, and he pushed me hard back against the door, and we moved, Peg . . . moved off down the drive . . .'

Peg stared at her, stared aghast. 'Kit, you're not going to tell me . . . you didn't have an accident! Kit, you're not trying to say . . .'

'We nearly ran a child down,' Kit said in a strangled voice, turning so white that Peg went to her and gripped her by the arm. 'It was a toddler in blue, a little girl. I'd noticed her at the reception. She was in the driveway, right in our path, playing with some sort of toy. Tim didn't see her, he wasn't looking, he was looking at me and laughing. I went crazy, I think, made a grab for the wheel just as the child moved. We careered past her, I could see her there, standing on the verge . . .'

'Good *lord*!'

'Tim stopped at the gates, I jerked on the handbrake and tore back to where we'd seen the child. She was playing with an engine, spinning the wheels round on the palm of her hand. She smiled at me, totally unconcerned. People came running—guests who'd seen the hair's-breadth escape she'd had. The first to reach us was a man I took to be her father . . .'

'The Niall man?'

'Yes, but of course I didn't know *who* he was then. All I knew was he'd turned on Tim and was flaying him with words. What he called him, what he said to him, was simply terrible, Peg! People were crowding round and listening, he just went on and on. Of course it was reaction, shock . . . he was very, very upset; so was the child's mother, she was hysterical. I stuck up for Tim, I was so incensed; he was in the wrong, I know, but I couldn't stand by and see him humiliated like that. He wasn't all that drunk, you know, only a little bit. He never intended to drive farther than the gates, he told me that afterwards. And in a way it was all my fault, I should have made quite sure that he gave me the keys when we got to the wedding. I ought to have taken them *then*.'

'With the benefit of hindsight, maybe you should have.' Privately Peg cursed Tim . . . or his memory; she had never liked him much. 'What happened then?' she prompted gently.

'Tim and I got back in the car, and I drove slowly home, feeling like death, feeling sick, still seeing that streak of blue as the child ran to safety, still seeing her mother's face.'

'And the father's, no doubt?'

'He wasn't the father,' Kit told her.

'Not?'

Kit shook her head. 'I found that out this afternoon, just now in the hospital foyer. Lots of us were waiting for the storm to pass, and I got talking to Charles Niall. He asked about Tim, and you know how it is, one thing leads to another. I asked him about his wife and child.'

'And he said it wasn't his child?'

'He said it wasn't his wife, either!'

Peg giggled, then sobered again. 'Just as well he *wasn't* married to such a dizzy woman! Fancy letting a little kid wander off with all those cars about!'

'Yes,' Kit agreed.

'Does he live in . . . at the hospital, I mean?'

'I've no idea—I shouldn't think so. Most registrars live out. I don't think he's been at the General long. Someone told me three months. That might be why I've not seen him around, that and the fact that I've been working out at Cawnford. He's noticeable enough, goodness knows,' Kit added, speaking half to herself.

Peg nodded, her attention straying. She had heard Bob's car turning in. So had Joe, who climbed on to a chair and waved excitedly as his father, hunched against the rain and turning up his collar, made a dash for the front door, just as Kit had done. Peg went to open it and the two embraced. Kit called out a greeting to Bob, then went into her sitting-room, taking Dee with her. Presently she heard the Carltons go upstairs.

It seemed a long time since she had welcomed a man home, made a meal for him, gone to bed with him, shared her life with him. She had married Tim when she was nineteen, during her second year of training. Very often she had been on duty when Tim came home from work, and vice versa, for he had tended to work very irregular hours. She envied Peg, she realised that. She could hear, as she sat there with Dee, the sounds of laughter from the room above, she could hear Joe's piping voice and Bob's deep brown one, interspersed with Peg's excited tones. She envied them, yet she knew she didn't want to marry again. 'We'll stay a one-parent family,' she said, stroking the top of Dee's head. 'I shall be sensible about you, and you'll want for nothing, certainly not for love.' Lifting the baby on to her lap, she played her favourite game of 'This little piggy' before her bath and bed.

None of the upstairs rooms had been changed when Peg and Bob moved in, but Kit had had an extra bathroom put in on the ground floor. She felt this was very necessary, especially with a baby; the new bathroom and Dee's room were en suite.

She had eaten her own light meal and was clearing away in the kitchen when Peg came down with her loaded tray of washing up to be done. 'Don't hurry, Kit, I can wait,' she said, watching her cousin rinsing the sink and hanging the tea-towel up. 'As a matter of fact,' she set the tray down with a bang on the pinewood table, 'I want to ask you a favour. Bob would rather I didn't, but all the same . . .'

'You're going to.' Kit stripped off her rubber gloves. 'If it's sitting in with Joe, you know I will, you don't have to ask.'

'It's not him, it's not Joe, it's something entirely different. Bob has asked a client here to supper on Thursday week. It's a woman client—Faith Melville from the Craft Shop in the High Street. Bob handles all her tax matters, and accounts, and things like that. She's got other shops too, one in Cheltenham and another in Newquay in Cornwall. Anyway, she's a valued client and he wants to ask her here. She'll be bringing a friend, so there'll be four of us all told.'

'Sounds all right . . . four's a good number.'

'Yes,' Peg looked unconvinced, 'but I'm not the world's best cook, am I?' Her round blue eyes met Kit's hazel ones. 'I'll never make the grade.'

'That's silly, Peg, of course you will. I'll help you, if you like.' Kit knew this was what Peg was really asking. She saw her face light up.

'Kit, you're an angel!'

'Yes, maybe, but I'm hardly Cordon Bleu.'

'Oh, you are, you are . . . you're a super cook, you're streets ahead of me. You're far more creative, you know you are. I don't want to let Bob down.'

'After so much flattery, I'm a push-over!' Kit gave her cousin a playful shove. 'Of course I'll help you . . . you can hire me for the whole of that day, if you like. I don't work on Thursdays, so no problem . . . a change is as good as a rest!'

'I'll do all the running around and clear up afterwards.' Peg squeezed detergent into the sink with so much enthusiasm that a cloud of tiny bubbles eddied round her head. She was five years older than Kit, but often appeared to be younger. Their mothers were sisters, and the two girls had always been close.

'Tell me more about Faith Melville. She's a trendy type, isn't she?' Kit had been in her shop, which was next door to Bob's thin office. He was sandwiched between the Craft Shop and an ironmonger's called Brads.

'Yes . . . arty-crafty, suits her shop . . . all high cheekbones and hair, and long skirts, everything flowing, tall and angular. She's older than me, well in her thirties and unmarried, I gather. I wonder why. Bob says she's very shrewd.'

'Shrewd enough to stay single,' said Kit, just as Peg swivelled round with a cry of:

'Oh, Kit, I *knew* there was something else I had to tell you! I saw Hugh MacBride today when I fetched Joe from play-school. I'd got Dee in the buggy, Joe at my side, and a whole load of shopping. He was climbing into his silver Jag outside the house at the end of the road here, the one with the monkey-puzzle tree in the front garden. There's a child there, I know. He was probably making a domiciliary visit. Consultants do that, don't they?'

'Yes. Did he see you?' asked Kit.

'Of course he did. He could hardly avoid it—we were only feet away. He spoke to us. Joe showed him his drawing, and Dee gave him one of her looks. He asked how you were, and I'm sure he wasn't simply being polite. He wanted to know, he waited for an answer. And, Kit, he looked superb! I don't think I've ever seen a man look so immaculate . . . the suit he had on must have cost the earth.'

'He always looked like that, even on the wards, with children crawling all over him.' Kit smiled a little, remembering Hugh . . . slim and sandy-bearded, an Edinburgh Scot who had made his way in the South.

Hugh was a consultant paediatrician and up until last month Kit had worked for him as a receptionist at his consulting rooms out at Cawnford. She had left him in order to take up her present nursing post at the General.

His manner had been curt when she took her leave of him. He had made her feel guilty, which she felt was unfair; he had made her conscience prick in a very uncomfortable manner whenever she thought of him. Yet she had given him proper notice, she hadn't let him down, and she had found someone to take her place, who had been there for some time. Of course he'd been kind to her, very kind, just when she needed help most, but surely that didn't mean, she had to stay with him for ever? After all, he had known she was a nurse.

Peg went upstairs, but Kit didn't hear her, she was thinking right back to when she and Tim had moved to Sussex, nearly two years ago. She had gone to a nursing agency then and obtained a post at St Margaret's, the big children's hospital out at the neighbouring town of Cawnford. After Tim was killed she continued to nurse there until her pregnancy forced her to stop. It was then that Hugh MacBride, whom she had sometimes accompanied on ward rounds, came to her rescue and asked her if she would care to work for him at his private consulting rooms, near to the hospital. 'The fact is,' he told her, 'I need someone at once. My nurse/receptionist has left. I know you can type, I've seen you helping Sister out on occasion. The fact that you're pregnant needn't matter at all . . . in a way it's rather fitting!' He tried to make her smile, and succeeded. She liked Dr MacBride, and was flattered to be offered a post which she knew most girls would have coveted. 'Think it over,' he urged her. 'We could try it and see how it works.'

She did so, and stayed with him until a month before Dee's birth. He then engaged a temporary girl for a little over three months, after which Kit went back to him; they were pleased to see one another. She was able to take Dee with her too, for Hugh MacBride's housekeeper 'minded' her while Kit got on with her work.

Hugh MacBride was a childless widower. His wife had been an invalid, who had developed a disease of the spinal cord early on in their marriage, and she died when he was a registrar at Great Ormond Street. All this he confided to Kit one day, and she told him about herself. Each liked and trusted the other, which made for pleasantness.

Hugh had taken Kit home one evening when her car was in for repair. He met Peg and small Joe, and also Kit's parents from Cannoch Moor in Scotland, who were staying at Hilldown at the time.

But their friendship was work-based; Hugh MacBride was a busy man, and Kit was a nurse, first and foremost a nurse, and as time went on she knew she had to get back to ward nursing, nothing else would satisfy. 'I'm trained for it, Hugh,' she tried to explain, 'I can't settle for anything else.' She very nearly said, 'anything *less*' . . . Hugh divined this at once, and said with a sense of personal affront that of course she must please herself. This marked the start of a new, chilly era, which was very uncomfortable. A few weeks later when Kit got her part-time post at the Bewlis General, she was glad to give in her notice, glad to leave Hugh's employ. It was a business arrangement and it finished, she gave him proper notice *and* found a successor . . . she hadn't let him down.

That night she dreamed about him. She was back at his house in Park Road, showing worried parents in and out, soothing fractious children, typing reports, answering the telephone. But somewhere in all this Charles Niall figured; he arrived at the house in a terrible state with a little girl who was very ill indeed. Kit let him in, and as she did so she saw that the child he carried—the child over which he was agonising—wasn't a stranger to her. It was her own baby.

The little girl was Dee.

CHAPTER THREE

WITH TEN of their twenty-four patients on their first post-operative day, the nursing staff on Bellingham Ward were frantically busy next morning. There was no outward sign of rush, the atmosphere was calm. There was no agitated bustling, yet every nurse on duty was working all out, passing at speed from one task to another, trying to remember a long list of jobs which simply had to be done. I shall never get through . . . I shall never get through . . . beat a frenzied refrain inside the white-coiffed head of every overworked 'angel'. Outside the sun poured down from a sky of peerless blue, laying a mantle of gold on the backs of the Downs.

Kit had an enormous pile of paperwork to get through. She was tackling this at the nurses' station —the central ward desk. She was filing intake and output charts when the ward doors opened and in filed a posse of doctors headed by the Professor. Their expected arrival had been yet another reason for the morning rush. They were here to do a full round—a teaching round, moreover—so they were likely to be in the ward for at least an hour.

The General was a large and well-known teaching hospital, and the creeper-covered medical school at the rear of the precinct looked out on to the old part of the town. Many a student had listened to a lecture, or swotted up his notes, with half his eye and attention on the towers of Bewlis Castle, which dated back to early Norman times.

Kit's eye continued to rest on the moving group at the doors. Sister Clive was a step behind the Professor; she was pushing the trolley of notes. At her side was Charles

Niall, rearing up, white coat hanging loose; behind him was the houseman, Dick Parker, behind him four medical students—their white coats were short, as befitted their lowly rank. Niall spoke to the student nearest to him, who promptly produced a notebook and jotted in it, dark head bent to his task. Charles Niall's hair, Kit observed, was the tough sort without any gloss, the sort that keeps tidy in a wind, yet seldom lies really flat. As his white coat swung open she glimpsed dark trousers and a pale blue shirt. His tie was askew across his chest; perhaps it had blown like that as he crossed the yard. He straightened it, as though he had caught her thought, or caught her staring . . . surely he hadn't. Embarrassed, she glanced away, but her mind's eye retained his image and projected it faultlessly on the squared graph paper in her grasp.

Professor Planner, the only one of the group who wore no white coat, marched ahead in his tight pinstripe, hands behind his back. Mrs Farley, the gastrectomy, was the first patient to be seen. The curtains were drawn round her bedspace and the crowd of medics filed in. It was enough to give her claustrophobia, thought Kit sympathetically, wondering as she did so what it would be like to lie in a high hospital bed and gaze blearily up into the face of Charles Niall, the registrar! I'd get well fast if it killed me, she muttered, then smiled at the Irish phrase which sounded, to say the least of it, decidedly absurd, coming from the lips of a girl who was half a Scot. And quite probably, if one *were* a patient, he might not be so stern. His features might soften to match his voice, which no one, but no one, could fault. She could hear it now—a rich baritone, contrasting so vividly with Professor Planner's throat-clearing, gravelly tones.

It was at this point that a third voice impinged on Kit's ear—a thin, weak, Cockney voice, and it came from the cholecystectomy patient in bed fourteen. Praying that she didn't want a bedpan, Kit went to her at once. She was probably uncomfortable, poor little woman; she had had her gall-bladder removed the previous morning, due to the presence of stones.

'I keep sliding down, Nurse, and I'm that sore . . . can you lift me up?' She had a face like a worried squirrel, her eyes were overbright. Kit turned down her bed-clothes and saw at once that her 'donkey'—the bolster wedge placed at the soles of her feet to stop her sliding down the bed—had moved out of position.

'We'll soon put that right,' she said. She summoned Learner Nurse Holden, who was coming out of the day-room, and between them they carefully lifted the patient and re-positioned the donkey, tucking the ends more firmly into place. 'How's that?' Kit shook up her pillows. The woman leaned back.

'Luvly, ducks . . . many thanks. Couple of angels, you are.'

'I wish we had angels' wings . . . we need 'em, practically all the time!' Jean Holden laughed, flapping her arms and pretending to soar away, just as the group of doctors all filed by.

'Who are *they*, then, a flamin' strike committee?' the patient said audibly. No one appeared to hear except Charles Niall, who walked the few steps to her bed.

'We're not striking today, Mrs Wrightson!' His long mouth twitched at the corners. It wasn't quite a smile, but it got very near one. 'How are you feeling?' he asked.

'I've felt better, sir.' She was suddenly weary.

'It's early days yet, you know.' He took her wrist, feeling for her pulse, noting her over-bright eyes. He glanced at her charts, then at her notes which he had filched from the trolley. 'If all is well by Saturday, we'll have a cholangiogram done,' he said sotto voce to Kit, turning away from the bed. 'Her pulse is fast, but not seriously so.' He broke off as Professor Planner screwed his neck round and gave a nod.

'Ready when you are, Charles.'

Kit returned to the desk, aware of having glimpsed yet another side to Charles Niall. He didn't talk down to the patients, nor hold himself aloof. His manner with them was therapeutic—humorous, and kind. I can't get over feeling wary of him . . . she struggled to file a report . . . but then I don't have to like him personally, only on the surface. Here, at the hospital, is the only place where we're ever likely to be in contact, and then only rarely, with Sister doing the honours most of the time. Then why should she feel that Sister was lucky? She must be going mad!

The telephone purred at her elbow, and immediately she was immersed in taking down details of Mrs Fanshawe's liver function tests. The pharmacist waved to her from the office, with a query about a prescription. By the time she had dealt with him and had a word with the dietician, sorted out a muddle with the laundry bags, and calmed down a social worker, the Professor and his team had left the ward.

The next time Kit saw Charles Niall was on Wednesday afternoon. It was shortly after two o'clock and Sister was at a conference, which meant that Kit was temporarily in charge of the ward. Visiting was between two-thirty and four, and by the time Charles Niall crossed the landing one or two visitors were already assembling in the corridor, trying to see through the portholes into the ward. Kit was in the office with the door standing ajar, in case any of the visitors might wish to speak to her. When the door was thrust open and she looked up to see Charles Niall there, her startled expression appeared, for a second, to reflect itself on his face. 'Oh, you're here again today, are you?' he said tactlessly . . . purposely tactlessly, Kit felt sure. Politely she rose to her feet. Resisting the urge to tell him she worked only one shift less per week than the full-time nurses, she looked at him straightly and said:

'Yes, Mr Niall, what can I do for you?'

'Where's Sister?' He shut the door and advanced towards the desk.

'Downstairs in conference with the SNO and the Chief Administrator. She should be back about four o'clock.' Kit sat down when he did. Why was he here? What did he want? He sighed, and it seemed to her that his swift expellation of breath had a speaking voice of its own—a voice which told her that he found Sister's absence the devil of a nuisance and the part-time nurse a doubtful substitute.

'I expect you know Mrs Bentick is going home this afternoon. I want to see her before she leaves.' His glance flicked away from Kit's face. He was looking past her, past her right ear, towards the big square window that gave an unobstructed view of the ward. 'I can't see her. Where is she . . . and where are her notes?'

'Her notes are here—I was just about to send them down to Records. Mrs Bentick is in the day-room, saying goodbye to her friends. Her husband is coming to fetch her.'

'I know. I want to see him as well. I want to warn him about her lifting heavy crates and boxes.' He watched Kit getting the notes from the drawer.

Alice Bentick and her husband had a small green-grocery business. John Bentick suffered from angina, which was why Mrs B. had taken on the heaving lifting work. Kit mentioned this to Charles Niall. 'Yes, yes, I know . . . it's all in here,' he tapped the folder of notes. 'Even so, they'll have to do something about it, get in some help for a time. That looks like Mr Bentick now.' He broke off as an overweight man lumbered past the first three beds, then stood by his wife's empty one. Mrs Bentick was looking out for him, and she hailed him from the day-room. He hurried towards her and she towards him; in the end they were nearly trotting. They embraced as though they had been apart for years.

'Better let them get that over first,' remarked Charles Niall in humourless tones. He had come round to Kit's side of the desk, and looking swiftly at him she saw that he was watching the Benticks walking hand in hand to the day-room, with a very strange expression on his face.

'They're a devoted couple,' she ventured quietly. 'I noticed them yesterday, when he came to visit.'

'In that case, Staff, he ought to take care of her.' Charles Niall's arm knocked against hers as he moved away from the window. His voice had hardened, so had his look, the impassiveness was back. What could have been a kind of yearning, an open-faced vulnerability, had vanished as though it had never been. And most likely I imagined it, Kit thought as she followed him out of the room.

'Your wife won't be able to do heavy work for three months at least,' said Charles Niall as he stood in front of the Benticks, long legs slightly apart.

'I'll see that she doesn't.' John Bentick picked up Alice's case.

'And *I'll* see that *he* doesn't!' Alice took it back, setting it down by her feet in order to shake Charles Niall's hand and thank him for all he had done for her.

'It's all part of the service, Mrs Bentick. Now, you do your part by sticking strictly to everything I've said. And remember to attend Outpatients next month, for your follow-up. Have you got your appointment card and the date?'

'Staff Nurse gave it to me.' Alice included Kit in her smile of thanks.

'Right then, I'll see you out.' Charles picked up her case, managing to do so with such sleight of hand that no one but Kit noticed. She watched the three of them crossing to the doors, Mrs Bentick in the middle, waggling her fingers in a goodbye gesture to the 'old lags' she was leaving. Charles said something to her and she laughed; he was still carrying the case. He wasn't above small acts like that, and he didn't withdraw himself—at least not from the patients, whom he saw as flesh and blood people, not just as bodies on which to operate.

The corridor had one or two late visitors sauntering down its length when Kit left the ward a little later, en route for the office again. It also had Charles Niall, coming back from the lifts. Roughly midway between him and Kit was a youth in jeans and trainers, carrying a bottle of orange squash. Having seen his photograph the day before, Kit knew who he was—Mrs Gartside's son David, from Barhampton, complete with Mohican haircut and hoop earrings which struck his neck as he walked. She stood outside the office door and waited for him to reach her, but he never did, for without any warning, apart from a lip-stretching smile, he crashed over backwards, straight as a rod, to the sound of crashing glass as the bottle of squash flew up and hit the wall.

Charles and Kit reached him simultaneously, just as he gave a cry and began to convulse, to twitch and jerk, to thresh about on the floor. 'Bring a towel, clear the corridor, close the ward doors!' Kit was almost unaware of issuing snap instructions to Nurse Geare who, with Rosa and Marylyn, had rushed out of the kitchen looking scared.

Charles was doing his best to hold the boy's head and tilt his jaw forward. 'A grand mal attack, by the looks of it.' Kit could hardly catch his words, due to David's stertorous breathing and the thumping and pounding of his arms and legs as he twisted about on the floor.

Jill Geare returned with a towel and Kit got the corner between David's teeth. 'He's bitten his tongue already, dammit!' Charles saw the trickle of blood.

'We could hardly have been quicker.' Again Kit was terse; the fit seemed to go on for hours. In fact it lasted less than five minutes, after which the strong contractions began to get weaker . . . and weaker . . . and weaker, until they finally ceased, and the boy slid into the comatose phase.

They lifted him into a side-ward, and up on to the bed. 'See if you can find Dr Manders, get him bleeped,' said Charles. He passed careful hands down the patient's limbs. 'No obvious injury, but until he's conscious and can say where it hurts, best to leave well alone.'

Carl Manders was bleeped, he telephoned the ward, and Charles told him what had happened. Within minutes David Gartside was being examined by the tall gaunt doctor, who specialised in disorders of the brain. David came round at the end of it all, he spoke, and complained of headache. He took the news that he had had a 'mild' fit with dazed, sluggish calm. 'Just tired . . . just tired.' He closed his eyes and fell into a natural sleep.

'I'll admit him to the observation ward, keep him in overnight. Meantime, perhaps you can get some kind of history from the mother,' Dr Manders suggested, looking over at Kit. A movement from the doorway made them all turn round. Mrs Gartside was there, her floral kimono flapping, matching shortie nightdress showing a fair amount of bandaged leg. Her eyes went to the boy on the bed.

'I knew it was Dave,' she said. 'I heard someone had fell down in a fit, and I knew it was my boy.' She limped in and Charles gave her a chair, as she blinked away starting tears. With one hand on her son's bed and the other clasping Kit's, she told them that David had been epileptic since he was four years old. 'He's on tablets for it, they keep him right, he's not had a fit for years, but he has to watch out—you know what I mean, he mustn't do dangerous things. P'raps it was coming in 'ere to see me that brought this seizure on. Dave don't like 'orspitals, I shouldn't have asked him to come. What will happen?' She looked at Kit, but it was Charles who explained that

David would be admitted to a ward downstairs for the night.

'He'll need to sleep it off, Mrs Gartside. He'll be very tired, you see.'

'Oh, I know how 'e'll be, sir . . . right as ninepence when 'e wakes up. I remember from the last time,' she looked at David and sighed. She longed to touch him, but didn't like to . . . not with the doctors there.

'Once I'm satisfied that he's fit to go home, perhaps your husband could fetch him,' Carl Manders suggested, folding his stethoscope. 'Now, can you give me the name of his home doctor, please?'

She did so, then Kit helped her up, to make way for the stretcher trolley, which was being wheeled in by the Casualty porters, who aligned it to the bed. 'These things happen so quick, don't they?' said Mrs Gartside, as her son was borne smoothly away, arms tucked under a blanket, his cockscomb haircut sticking out like a brush.

As both Charles Niall and Dr Manders appeared to be making their exit, Kit took Mrs Gartside back into the main ward. 'I shouldn't have arsked him to come and see me, it must have been 'ot in that bus.' Mrs Gartside drank the tea Kit brought her, but without her usual zest, and she left the cake. 'I think it would choke me,' she explained.

Kit stayed with her for a few minutes, trying to be comforting. 'David has done well to go so long without a fit. The fact that he's had one today might mean that his tablets need adjusting. What work does he do?'

Mrs Gartside brightened. 'Oh, 'e don't work, dear. 'E's still at school, takes his A-levels soon, going to be a teacher—my Dave's the clever one. I tell him he'll 'ave to do something about his 'air very soon. I don't know why he thinks he 'as to freak 'isself out like that.'

Kit excused herself. She had just seen Charles Niall standing in the office. The white-coated bulk of him seemed to fill the viewing window. She hadn't expected him to come back; had he been waiting long? She left the ward, not exactly running, but moving at a brisk pace. When she went into the office he was over by the cabinets, riffling through one of the drawers. 'I'm very pushed for time, Staff,' he said testily. 'I didn't bargain on being sidetracked, I'm due in Outpatients at three.'

'Were you wanting to see . . .' she began, feeling hot.

'Miss Phipps, and I want her notes.'

'They're here on the desk,' she gave them to him. 'Would you like to see her now?'

'In a minute.' He found the treatment sheet and studied the last three items. Looking at him, standing there, chin wedged down on his chest, breathing impatiently and looking cross, Kit felt her own composure crack a little and knew she should exercise care. But his attitude, what he had said, and the strain of the past half hour, caused a small flame of anger to flicker inside her, making her burn to tell him that she was so *sorry* the Gartside boy had had the temerity to fall down in a grand mal fit only paces in front of him. She was so *sorry* he'd been sidetracked, baulked and hindered like that, and made late for his three o'clock clinic . . . what a terrible thing that was! Oh yes, she longed to say all that and a great deal more, but old habits die hard, and members of the nursing profession do not . . . not ever, however provoked . . . spit venom at senior doctors; so she held her tongue, kept her cool, and her chagrin under wraps. But her face was crimson, and Charles Niall saw it, as he closed the notes at last. He looked at her, then looked again. 'Anything wrong?' he asked. But he made the enquiry so carelessly, with such absence of concern—as though her answer didn't matter, but he might as well hear what it was—that Kit was impelled to say what she did, while managing with a great effort to remember his rank and not let the words already filling her mouth to burst out, to come out with too much of a rush.

In controlled tones, therefore, even cold tones, she told him she could have coped with all the trauma of David's fit. Nurse Geare would have aided her. 'It was good of you to stop and help, Mr Niall, but you needn't have done so, you know. I'm familiar with epileptiform attacks, most nurses are. I could have managed, *you* could have carried on!'

There was a long, ticking, pregnant moment in which they both stood and stared . . . he at her, she at him; he opened and closed his mouth. 'I don't normally step over sprawling bodies as though they're not there,' he told her. 'As to your ability to cope, that was obvious to me during the first five seconds of the poor little devil's attack. Now, as I don't want to delay any longer, *may* I see Miss Phipps?'

'Yes, I . . . yes.' Kit felt blown off course, completely at a loss. She didn't know whether to cling to her wrath as a necessary defence, or let it go and abandon herself to the little slip of pleasure that his words of praise . . . although faint . . . had brought about.

He was walking to the door, and she followed. He held it open for her, but before she could make a move to go out Sister Clive stepped in. She smiled at them both. 'All right, Staff, thanks, I'll take over now. Good afternoon, Mr Niall.' Her glance passed from Kit to him.

'Ah, Sister . . . splendid,' he said. 'Now perhaps we can get on.' Leaving Kit half in and half out of the office, they made their way to the ward and through the doors.

Rosa and Marylyn had made a good job of clearing up David Gartside's smashed-to-smithereens bottle of orange squash. Only the faintest of smears was visible on the pale green wall, and only one speckle of glass, the size of a crumb, winked up at Kit from the vinyl floor. Thank goodness, she thought, as she picked it up, tomorrow's my non-working day. Tomorrow she would devote her energies to Dee and to home matters. She might even manage a walk on the Downs and let the southerly wind, blowing in from the English Channel twelve miles distant, straighten her thoughts into sensible shape again.

CHAPTER FOUR

DAVID Gartside went home on Friday. His father came to fetch him—a squat, dark-skinned little man, who kept reminding his son that he would have to lose a day's pay, 'just to come here for you.'

They went along to Bellingham Ward to see Mrs Gartside, and even though it was lunchtime, Sister let them go in. Kit was supervising the lunches, so she was able to speak to them, but she had to look at David twice before she was sure it was him. His stand-up hairstyle had wilted and lay on his scalp in bands; he had removed his earrings and put on spectacles, and the overall new effect was that of a student with a tendency to spots. Kit found the metamorphosis, for it was more than a simple change, a little sobering, especially when he shook her hand and thanked her, 'for seeing to me and everything . . . couldn't have been much fun.'

'If you had to be taken ill, David . . . *temporarily* ill,' she smiled, 'you couldn't have chosen a better spot for it. I enjoyed looking after you. I'm glad you're feeling better now. Good luck with your exams.'

'You're a nice girl,' Mrs Gartside told her, after the two had gone. 'You were good to Dave, real nice . . . what you said was just right. And his dad's not the bad-tempered bloke he seems, you know. He'll look after Dave all right, till I get out of 'ere. He don't show 'is best side, he's afraid of being thought soft.'

We all wear masks of a kind, Kit thought, as she moved away from the bed. We don't show ourselves as we really are, except to our nearest and dearest. We're afraid of hurt and ridicule. What a complex lot we are! Crossing over to bed fourteen, she helped Mrs

Wrightson drink some soup from a spouted feeding cup.

Mrs Gartside was discharged three days later. She went home in the sitting-up ambulance, together with nine other patients all discharged that day. Some lived in the immediate suburbs, some in outlying villages. By the time Mrs Gartside was helped into her semi-detached at Barhampton, there was only one patient left—an old man with emphysema. 'It's like ten little nigger boys this morning, Jock,' the driver said to his mate, who was crossing the verge and stepping on board again.

Kit caught only glimpses of Charles Niall during that week—once when she accompanied a patient down to theatre block, once in the yard, talking to Dr Sparrow from Haematology, and once turning out of the main gates in his green Audi car. On the last occasion he had seen her and raised an acknowledging hand. She had been with Dick Parker, who told her that Charles had a flat in Castle Close.

'How do you get on with him?' asked Kit as they mounted the steps and walked across the hall to the line of lifts.

'All right, so far. He's a good surgeon, the strong silent type. He doesn't go in for a load of chat as some surgeons do, you know. They ramble on about their golf, or moan about the government all the while they're probing around in some poor blighter's guts. The most we get from Niall is a quiet . . . 'All right at your end, Doctor' or 'You're in my light, move, will you' or . . . 'OK, you can close'. The theatre staff like him, he's the kind of man who grows on you gradually—on the males, that is. On the women he seems to make an instant impact. How do you find him?' Dick enquired, stepping into the lift.

'I don't see him all that much.' The lift soared up to Level three—the Surgical floor, and Kit and Dick got out.

'That's a *very* cagey reply, Staff Nurse!'

'But perfectly true,' Kit laughed, watching Dick cross the landing to Kilross which was men's surgical. The Professor was on holiday, which was why Dick Parker was doing most of the ward rounds; Charles was in theatre for the greater part of each day.

Bellingham was busy, for as soon as a patient went out another came in. Quite often there was less than a day's overlap, just time for the bed-frame and mattress to be sponged and dried, the clothes made into a pack. When Kit went off duty on Wednesday—the day before Bob's dinner-party—both side-wards were occupied, which was fairly unusual. A patient with a goitre was in the first one, while the second was occupied by a deaf woman in her early forties, who lip-read so well that no one had to use sign language, or the special diagrammed cards. She was on Charles's list for surgery on Friday. A hiatus hernia had been making life increasingly difficult for her. She was thankful, she said, to be in hospital.

Kit and Peg decided to get their shopping done early next morning. With Dee strapped into her seat in the back of the Austin Metro, Joe bouncing about at her side, and the buggy in the boot, they proceeded down Mount Cliff Road and into Firle End Drive where the play-school was held, and Joe was dropped off, much to his delight. He hated shopping and Dee wasn't yet of an age to be very much fun for a vigorous little boy of four years old.

They bought avocados, jumbo prawns, the plumpest duck they could find, fresh peas, courgettes, new potatoes, and wine. They bought three kinds of cheese and two kinds of grapes, and Blue Mountain coffee beans. 'We'll be ruined!' said Peg cheerfully, as weighed down with plastic bags they made their way to the car park at the far end of the town. As they passed Bob's office his secretary could be seen, just a shape behind frosted glass, pounding away at her typewriter, one of the manual sort. Next door was the Craft Shop and inside they could see the wandy form of Faith Melville arranging a set of Toby jugs on a shelf. Her shop was attractive, two seascape paintings were displayed in the right-hand window; the other had tapestries with wools and silks spilling over a chair. The effect was simple, yet eye-catching; people were turning to stare.

'Who is she bringing tonight?' asked Kit, later that afternoon. She and Peg were in the kitchen preparing the food for cooking. Dee was crawling about on the floor, Joe was in the garden putting a worm into his seaside pail. 'But perhaps you don't know.' She wondered why her cousin wasn't answering.

'Oh yes, I know, and I was going to tell you, this morning . . . in the High Street.' Peg's voice came over jerkily,

'Do I know him?' asked Kit.

'It's Charles Niall.'

'Oh, *no*, Peg!' Kit's knife clattered on to the floor.

'Yes, well, there it is. I knew you wouldn't be pleased. To have someone you don't especially like turn up on your doorstep is a bit much, and I told Bob so.' Peg's glance was troubled.

'I neither like nor dislike him, actually.' Kit retrieved her knife. She had been chopping onion, and she returned to it vigorously, making resounding bangs. 'Fancy him knowing Faith Melville,' she said.

Peg switched the food mixer on.

'I don't find that so surprising.' She was choosing her words. 'She's a fascinating woman, and having a shop in the centre of the town makes her prominent, puts her on show, makes her available. I expect Charles Niall went into buy something and, bingo, the rest followed. He's personable, you say?'

'Very—yes.' The onion was getting to Kit, her eyes stung, and she gave an unfeminine sniff.

'You don't mind all that much, do you, Kit?' Peg looked anxiously at her.

'No . . . there's no reason why I should.'

'Good.' Peg met her look.

'Does he know I live here?' asked Kit.

'I would think so, yes. You see, when Faith Melville told Bob that she was bringing a doctor from the General, Bob, naturally enough, said that you nursed there and mentioned Bellingham Ward. She in her turn is bound to have mentioned that to Dr Niall.'

'Mr . . . he's a surgeon,' Kit corrected, leaning against the table. Her gaze wandered round the kitchen; the news was just sinking in. He was coming here tonight . . . good heavens, *tonight*! . . . here, to her house! True, he'd be upstairs in the flat, but even so, under her roof, and she, Kit Tennant, would be cooking for him, *and* for his trendy girlfriend. 'Well, all I hope is they like roast duck!' She dragged the bird towards her and covered its chilly nakedness with foil.

'Duck,' said Dee from the doorway. She was having a whale of a time, scudding down the kitchen steps on her rear, climbing up on all fours. 'Duck, duck.' She liked the word, and repeated it incessantly. Her mother sighed and looked at the kitchen clock.

When Bob got home just after six both children were in bed. His wife was dressing, and his cousin-by-marriage was looking decidedly fetching in a low-waisted dress of almond green silk. No way did Kit intend to meet Charles Niall and Faith Melville wearing a pinny; she would put that on afterwards. She didn't want to meet them at all, but had agreed to Peg's suggestion that she should join them upstairs for a pre-dinner drink. 'They know you live here, it'll look so odd if you don't put in an appearance.' This was true enough, so of course she had said she would.

'Now remember,' said Bob, 'Peg and I will do all the fetching and carrying. Just load the trays and put them on here, and we'll do the rest.' He pointed to the end of the kitchen table, which was so closely cluttered that a single fork would have had to jostle for room. 'I still feel you shouldn't be doing all this,' he added, as he turned round.

'Think nothing of it.' Kit was arranging the starter course on plates—prawns and sliced avocados with creamy Roquefort dressing. 'I like cooking, I'm enjoying all this. I wouldn't do it if I didn't.'

'No, of course not.' Still looking worried, which he very often did, Bob made his way upstairs to shower and change.

Faith and Charles arrived on foot just after seven. Bob let them in, he was hovering in the hall. Kit remained where she was at the foot of the stairs, but as Peg came flying down to greet her guests, she drew her forward. 'You both know my cousin Kit.'

'I have that pleasure,' said Charles urbanely, and Kit suppressed a start. Had he got his tongue in his cheek, she wondered, or was this the social man? Was this the way he was, or could be, when out for the evening? Was this yet *another* side to him?

'You've been to my shop, I'm quite sure,' said Faith as they went upstairs, Bob leading the way, Kit and Faith following Charles and Peg behind.

'Yes, I have, and I always enjoy looking round it,' Kit answered pleasantly. Faith's ankle-length skirt was taffeta, it whispered as she climbed, up and up, from stair to stair, the swishing sound filled Kit's ears. Even so it didn't quite blot out the soft, blunted thud of Charles's footfalls close behind her heels. How well did they know one another? she wondered. What was their relationship? No business of hers . . . Bob opened the sitting-room door.

The sitting-room was attractive, with a big bay window overlooking the garden at the back. The ceiling had plaster mouldings, the décor was light, Peg's three-piece suite had Sanderson covers, a Steinway piano stood at the far end; Bob was musical. They would be eating in a similar but smaller room, just across the landing; Kit had helped Peg with the table earlier on.

Bob handed round drinks, and little flurries of talk got under way. 'This is a lovely room,' Charles remarked, from his seat on the sofa. Faith was beside him, her long black skirt pooling the tufted carpet. She had pulled her pale gold hair into a coil at the back of her head and the severe style showed off her beautiful bones. She was heavily made up, and completely relaxed, drinking vodka and lime.

'The Victorians knew how to build houses,' said Bob.

Charles agreed with him. 'I'm a flat-dweller at the moment,' he smiled briefly at Faith.

'I sublet my flat to Charles,' she explained, 'when I moved in over the shop. I like to be on the premises, and Castle Close, for him, is convenient for the hospital.' Her hand touched his dark-trousered knee. 'But weren't you lucky,' and this time her glance moved across to Kit, 'weren't you lucky to get a flat here in this house, with your cousins . . . but perhaps you managed to pull a few strings for her?' Her eyes questioned Bob, who was frowning into his glass.

'It wasn't like that, Miss Melville,' said Peg.

'Oh, please call me Faith.'

'It wasn't like that, Faith,' Peg began again, but was interrupted by Bob.

'Hilldown belongs to Kit,' he explained. 'She and her husband bought it two and a half years ago. Kit leased us this upper portion when Tim died—and believe me, we were only too glad to get it.'

'To be able to let it to my own family made all the difference,' said Kit. 'The thought of complete strangers upstairs was a little worrying.'

'And we absolutely love living here.' Peg spoke in breathy jerks.

'Peg and Kit are more like sisters,' explained Bob, 'they help one another out.'

'Like, for instance, tonight.' Peg was determined to have her say. 'Kit has done all the cooking, she's super at that sort of thing.'

'And Peg is good at baby-minding, she copes with my small daughter, for four days in every week.' Kit set down her sherry glass.

'While you go out to work, you mean?' Faith smiled dazzlingly; she had perfect teeth that went with the rest of her.

'While I do my nursing job, yes,' Kit smiled back; then felt Charles's eyes upon her. She met them boldly, with a hint of challenge; he glanced away, looking bland. No man could look more *smooth* than he, be more annoyingly silent at a time when a heartening remark like, 'What a good arrangement,' would have made all the difference to the way she was feeling, which was very much odd man out.

Peg had got hiccoughs, Kit could hear her trying to stifle them; the clock on the mantelshelf chimed the half-hour—thank goodness she could go. 'If you'll please excuse me,' she rose to her feet, and so did Bob and Charles. Bob reached the door first, and opened it for her. 'Peg will be down in a minute,' he muttered straight into her ear—he wasn't very tall. Over his shoulder Kit could see Charles sitting down again.

'How old is your little boy, Peg?' she heard Faith asking, then the door closed and the group was lost to sight. And *well* lost. Kit sped down the stairs, thankful to have escaped. The kitchen received her like a haven, cooking smells and all. And no one, but no one, is going to get me up there again tonight, she vowed, as she garnished the golden-brown, done-to-a-turn duck with fresh orange segments and watercress sprigs.

The stairs journeys began some twenty minutes later, Peg and Bob working in perfect unity. They were full of praise for Kit's efforts when, after the main course was done, they came down with the dishes and remains. 'It was good enough for the Ritz,' enthused Peg, 'they both tucked in, even the skin-and-bone Faith Melville! God knows how she keeps like that. And as for your Charles . . . well, I've never been more surprised in my life! He's nothing like you led me to think. He's amusing, he kept us in fits. I don't wonder Faith can't keep her hands off him—he's certainly got what it takes.'

'I'm glad you like him,' said Kit quietly, getting the sorbets out. Peg wanted her to have coffee upstairs with them, and tutted when she refused.

'Well, I hope you've had your own supper, Kit,' she said at the foot of the stairs. 'I know what you are about skimping meals. I hope you've managed something.'

'I've been picking at tasty morsels all evening, and given myself indigestion,' laughed Kit, rubbing her chest, 'so I think I'll stay down here. In any case, Dee has been grizzling.'

'Excuses, excuses!' Peg tutted again, but didn't argue the point.

Later, when all the perambulations up and downstairs had ceased, when the party had repaired to the sitting-room . . . Kit heard them cross the landing and close the door . . . she decided to start clearing up. Peg had said not to, but Kit doubted if any self-respecting cook could leave a kitchen in the state hers was and not feel a sluttish slob. For a second, though, she was tempted to do so, for Dee was wailing again. She crossed the hall to the bedroom to try to calm her down.

Dee had eleven teeth and had started to cut her back ones. They were giving her trouble and she needed, at times, that special brand of comfort called TLC, which is tender, loving care. Seeing how miserable she was, Kit lifted her out of her cot. She was snugly clad in her sleeping suit. 'I'll take you through to the kitchen, poor little mouse!'and Dee snuffled into her neck.

The move was successful; the kitchen was warm, it was Dee's favourite place. She loved the noise the dishwasher made, she forgot about her sore gums. Finding a paper bag on the floor, she tore it into shreds . . . rip, rip, rip, rip . . . she beamed up at her mother, tears drying on her chubby face.

Busy wiping down the table and work-tops, and with her transistor turned on, Kit failed to hear the door open and all but jumped out of her skin when a voice said: 'Oh, good, I thought I might have got thc wrong door.' It was Charles Niall; well, who else? There he stood in her kitchen, holding the tray of used coffee things, smiling and looking pleasant and a shade embarrassed. 'Am I too late with these?'

'No, you're not, thank you. I wouldn't have risked them in the washer, anyway. I'll soon rinse them. Thank you for bringing them down.'

'Can I help?' he offered.

'Oh no, it's quite all right.' Kit took the tray from his hands. How stupid it was to feel so awkward, and to act awkwardly too. One of the cups toppled sideways, as she placed the tray on the drainer. She saved it in the nick of time, hoping he hadn't noticed. She turned róund, wondering why he didn't go.

'The others are talking business,' he said, 'or shop . . . in its literal sense.' He looked at Kit in her straight green dress that suited her copper-gold hair; he noticed the plastic yellow apron, which she had vowed she wouldn't be caught in, with COLMAN'S MUSTARD lettered across its front. Last of all he noticed Dee, who crawled out from under the table: 'Good heavens! Is this . . . ?' He stared at her.

'Meet Delia Christine Tennant!' Kit welcomed the diversion her daughter had made, as she went forward and picked her up.

'But she's still a baby!' His look was one of total surprise.

'She'll soon be a year, she was born eight months after Tim had his accident.' Kit didn't have to explain so exactly, but she did so just the same. 'She was . . . *is* . . . our first child,' she added for good measure.

'I see,' he nodded, looking over at them both, but he didn't speak to Dee, nor make any comment about her, other than his first one. Most people enthused about her, but Charles Niall wasn't most people. Feeling slighted on the baby's behalf, Kit set her back on the floor. 'It must have been a harrowing time,' he said as she straightened up.

'I had masses of help.' She stripped off her apron and laid it over a chair. 'I carried on doing paediatric nursing out at Cawnford for as long as I could. Then one of the consultants, Dr MacBride, offered me a post at his consulting rooms, as receptionist-nurse, even though I was heavily pregnant. I carried on with that both before and after Delia was born until April when I landed my part-time post at the General Hospital.'

'Didn't you want to stick to paediatrics?' he raised a dun-coloured brow.

'No, I didn't. I like children, but prefer nursing adults. I did surgical nursing in Kent, where we lived before we came here. I was glad to get back to it, and I'm very much enjoying being at the General.'

He nodded, but once again missed his cue for paying a compliment. He wasn't that kind of man, Kit decided, he didn't make pretty speeches. In some respects he was taciturn, or as Dick Parker had said, the strong, silent, implacable type—unless he was blazing with anger, like that time at Hampstead, nearly three years ago. 'I've met Hugh Macbride—he's a dedicated man,' he broke in, scattering her thoughts.

'He is . . . he loves children.'

'Just as well, I should think . . . they being his livelihood.'

The remark was a little two-edged, thought Kit, with her eye on Dee. She was crawling over the floor to Charles, circling round his feet, moving in closer, lifting each trouser-leg and taking a peep at his socks. Kit laughed, so did Charles, but he made no move to bend down to the child. 'She has your hair,' he observed, 'but she's not like you otherwise.'

'She has my hair and Tim's eyes.' Kit moved her away from his shoes. She lifted her up, and Dee yelled with frustration, making a terrible din. 'She's teething, she's not at her best,' Kit explained, disliking the fact that she felt she had to excuse her behaviour. What was it about Charles Niall that made her feel habitually on test? Clutching the baby, trying to calm her, she took her to the window where by sheer luck, sitting on top of the red brick garden wall was the next-door cat, washing its face in the dusk. Enthralled at the sight, Dee ceased her roars, so suddenly that the silence was a small shock, like instant deafness, till other sounds came through. They were floating down from the upstairs flat.

'Where on *earth* has Charles got to?' they heard in a voice that could only belong to Faith.

'Seems I've been missed.' He opened the door. Kit saw the relief on his face, or thought she did as he turned round and asked her if she was coming.

'No, I think not, not with this little nuisance,' she smiled at him over Dee's head.

He looked at the child, really looked at her this time; her coy smile made him laugh. 'I think,' he said, 'that her name should have been Delilah, not Delia. She's an enchantress, like her mother,' and he touched the baby's cheek.

Kit was still reeling from the shock of this compliment when he paid her another. 'The meal you cooked us was first-rate. I would like to say thank you. Good night, my dear.' He turned and went upstairs.

CHAPTER FIVE

Kit's birthday fell on a Friday two weeks later. No one at the hospital knew about it, so there were no sung greetings when she went on duty—not that she minded that. There was too much to do, too much work to get through, to concentrate on a birthday. And although twenty-five was in no way old, it wasn't the first flush of youth, or so she reasoned, in the stuffy warmth of the starch-smelling linen room, as she counted out bedding and piled it up in his arms.

In the corridor she was intercepted by Sister, who frowned at her over the sheets. 'Oh, leave those, Staff,' she said, 'Nurse Holden can cope with the beds. I want you to do the Stenson girl's dressing and take out her stab-drain. Mr Niall thinks the risk of peritonitis is minimal now; both he and the Prof saw her during the round.'

The round had just finished and the Professor and his team had gone into Kilross Ward. 'I thought they'd never get finished, Staff, and the *mess* they've made of the notes!' Sister threw up her hands and whisked into her office, leaving Kit to find Jean Holden and set her on making up the bed in the first of the two side-wards; Miss Creadie, the deaf patient, had been discharged.

Sighing a little, for June Stenson wasn't easy, Kit went to the clinical room, washed and dried a dressing trolley, and proceeded to lay it up. Before wheeling it into the ward, however, she went along to see June, to explain exactly what she intended to do.

June Stenson was only seventeen, five foot nothing and jockey weight. She had been thrown from her horse, which had reared in fright from the sound of a backfiring car, and one of its hooves had come down on her abdomen, rupturing her liver. She had been rushed into Downlands on Tuesday afternoon when the Professor, aided by Charles, had repaired the damage and drained the area. Biliary peritonitis had been the main worry at first, but now, although still very weak, June was doing well. She no longer needed blood transfusions, she could sit out of bed for a time, and was able to take light food orally. Partly due to her illness, but mainly due to nature, she was difficult to the point of rudeness, especially with the nurses, whom she treated as servants, but they bore her attitude well.

'Feel free,' she said unsmilingly, when Kit told her about her tube. Her bed, for easier nursing, was just inside the doors. She watched Kit go out, then return minutes later, wearing a mask and gown, and pushing a trolley; the curtains were pulled round the bed.

'You'll feel heaps better once this is done.' Kit unfolded the wrapper of the dressing pack and laid the contents out. She anticipated fuss and fidgeting from the spoiled young girl, but in this she was wrong, for June kept perfectly still as the tube site was swabbed, as the sterile pin was gently removed, as the tube itself was gripped with artery forceps and drawn firmly and easily out. 'All done.' Kit straightened up, smiled briefly at June, then completed the dressing and made her comfortable. 'I'll get you a cup of tea,' she said, pulling down her mask.

'I'll have fruit juice.' June's glance moved to the covered jug on her locker.

'I'll pour you some.'

The girl's face tightened. 'Oh, for God's sake leave me alone! I can get it when I want it, can't I . . . I'm not bloody paralysed! You've done what you came for, now naff off . . . I'm sick to death of this place!'

'I'm on my way,' said Kit with restraint, flicking the curtains aside. And she wasn't best pleased to see

Charles Niall on the other side of them, less than a yard distant, looking over at June.

'Better now?' he asked her, sarcasm thick in his voice, but lost on June, who smiled at him and looked instantly beautiful.

'All the better for seeing you, twice in one morning . . . terrific!'

She was met with total silence and he didn't return her smile. As Kit left the bedside so did he; he followed her out of the ward. 'You don't have to put up with that kind of thing, not even from a patient,' he said as they halted outside Sister's door.

'Oh well,' Kit shrugged, 'so what . . . it's all in a day's work. The main thing is she's getting well, and she's not always difficult. Her behaviour was nothing less than model all the time I was doing her dressing. She's not a bad kid on the whole, and she *has* been very ill.'

'Are you always so forbearing?' His glance was compelling; she looked at him, feeling warm. She tugged at the neck of her calico gown, as her mind went back to the time when she had stood in a hotel drive and harangued him for daring to be rude to Tim. She hadn't been forbearing then and neither, with reason, had he. Perhaps he was thinking of that time now; she was almost sure he was. His eyes were a glinty blue and taunting; she let his question pass.

'Do you want to see Sister, Mr Niall?' Kit was glad to look away and give a nod of thanks to Jean Holden who was relieving her of the trolley and taking it away to dirty utility. But she watched its departure with a sense of mild panic, feeling extra vulnerable without its chromium rail beneath her palms.

'What I want,' he said, 'is to sign the prescriptions. I forgot them earlier. Dick Parker's off till tomorrow, some of the scripts are urgent. Sister's not in her office, I've just looked, and I can't find the pad. Perhaps you know where . . .' As he spoke he began to walk into the office. Kit, following closely behind him glimpsed flowers on the desk, cellophane-wrapped, for a patient, of course, most probably for June. 'These are for you,' he said with abruptness, placing them in her arms—white roses, white carnations, white satin ribbon. They were lovely . . . so lovely. For one mad moment she thought they were from him. An astonished 'thank you' sprang to her lips, but before she could give it utterance, he pointed quickly to the card. 'I found them here on the desk, when I came in a few minutes ago, searching for the pad.'

'It's my birthday.' She sat down, collapsed down, more like, and opened the envelope holding the tiny card. She had nearly, oh so nearly, made a fool of herself. Had Charles guessed she thought they might be from him? Almost certainly he had. And the awful thing was she wished they were . . . she didn't care who had sent them, if he had not, and the knowledge shocked her. She must be losing her wits! She got out the card with trembling fingers and read the handwritten message: 'All the best for your birthday, Hugh MacBride'. 'They're from Dr MacBride.' She had to say something, so she told him who had sent them. She told him quite deliberately; he had his back to her.

'So your erstwhile employer has remembered your birthday!' He turned round from the window, squinting in the dazzle of sun on a glass-fronted bookcase.

'It's Hugh's birthday too.' Kit hadn't forgotten it, but had done nothing about it. She hadn't dared, hadn't felt he would want her to.

'I hope you sent *him* a bouquet,' Charles said in jocular tones.

The facetious remark wasn't worthy of comment. Kit looked at the flowers again, and as she did so her feelings about them imperceptibly changed. The occasion of her birthday had been marked by a gift from a man whom she very much liked. It was all the more welcome because she thought he had washed his hands of her . . . out of vexation because she had left his employ. The flowers were Hugh's version of an olive branch, she felt fairly sure about that, and she knew she would grasp it, she knew she would clutch it. She would ring him up and thank him for his super gift, just as soon as she got the chance.

A cough from the desk made her jump and sit up, then stand up, clutching her flowers. 'I'm sorry to gatecrash into your dreams,' Charles said with a twist to his mouth, 'but may I just bring to your notice that I managed to find the pad, that I've signed the prescriptions, and these are they!' He waved them aloft, then settled them under the glass crocodile Sister used as a paperweight.

'I wasn't much help, was I?' said Kit, feeling a fool.

'Not a lot, no.' He walked round the desk and stood in front of her. 'Still, on this auspicious day you're allowed a little latitude,' he touched the flowers. 'Better put those in water before they wilt, or drop, or whatever it is that flowers do.'

'Yes, I'm going to.'

As his hand fell to his side his fingertips brushed her arm. The contact was small, was fleeting, was less than featherlight, yet a current of feeling shot through her, so sharply and shockingly that she felt he must see its effect on her face. He hadn't moved an inch. He was standing stock still, she could hear his breathing; she stared at the white lapels of his linen coat, at the brown of his throat, and felt bolted into the floor. Then he moved—he moved first, and her view of him changed as he turned round in a rush, spinning the door wide, making a draught, causing the metal handle to crash against the wall and make a mark. 'Enjoy the rest of your birthday,' he said outside in the passage. He left the door for Kit to close, for her to lean against, till she got her breath back and told herself that a flash of physical feeling for a man as attractive as Charles Niall was entirely natural. It was natural and not worth worrying about, not even worth very high rating, not when she didn't even like him; she must be in a bad way to hit the ceiling at the merest brush of his hand!

Soon after this the news leaked out that it was Staff Nurse Tennant's birthday. Marylyn and Rosa had a whip-round and bought a cake in their lunch hour. Nurse Geare got a card from the hospital shop and all the staff on the ward signed it, and presented it, while Sister turned a blind eye to the number of trips her nurses were making to the small ward kitchen where against-the-rules tea was brewed and the cake was cut.

When Kit got home there were parcels to open. Peg had put them in the sitting-room. She and the children came down to share in the fun of discovering what they were and who they might be from. There was a cheque from Kit's parents in Cannoch Moor in Scotland; a Fair Isle cardigan from her grandparents who lived near them; chocolates and tights from Aunt Beth, Peg's mother in Surrey; while her parents-in-law had sent her a handbag and a cuddly toy for Dee. There were several cards and letters from friends, and all the while Kit was reading them Peg was exclaiming over and arranging Hugh's flowers in a vase. 'These must have cost an absolute bomb!' She was very, very impressed.

'Yes, I know. I must ring up and thank him.' Kit put down a long letter from Harriet Tennant, her mother-in-law, who wanted to come and see her in the near future. Kit dreaded the thought of it. 'If I ring now, before six o'clock, I might just catch him,' she told Peg, going through into the hall.

There was a nervous feel about ringing Hugh, a feeling that worsened as she spun the dial and spoke to the new secretary/nurse, who had finished work and was packing up to go home. Within seconds Hugh's quick, light voice, with the faintest of Edinburgh accents, came floating over the wires, straight into her ear. She wished him a happy birthday and mentioned the flowers. 'I appreciate them so much . . . it was such a lovely surprise.'

His enquiries as to how she and Dee were, how she was liking her job, were got over very quickly. He was going, Kit was sure, to ring off at any second, but in that she was proved to be wrong: 'Katherine,' he said, 'if you don't happen to be going out this evening, I wonder if you would have dinner with me, to celebrate our birthday. I know it's short notice, but another evening would lack the same sense of occasion.'

'Yes, it would,' said Kit, playing for time, and trying to keep the note of surprise out of her voice, for surprised she certainly was. During the time she had worked for Hugh, he had never asked her out. There had been shared moments over coffee and tea, discussions about the patients, and as time went on they had talked about themselves and found common ground. But the relationship had ended there . . . there had been no follow-up. She had never wanted there to be one, and she wasn't sure she did now. For one thing she was feeling jaded, distinctly under par. Rosa's cake, eaten in snatches, wasn't suiting her inside. She was also tired, bone tired . . . what she wanted most of all was to get into her leisure suit, curl up on the settee, and watch television, with something on a tray. But perhaps she ought to make an effort; she ought not to give way to such unimportant feelings as tiredness and mild indigestion. She was getting old before her time . . . she must pull herself together. She said 'yes' to Hugh, and heard his satisfied grunt.

Peg was pleased, her face lit up. 'I could see this coming,' she said. 'That day I saw him here in our road, when he asked how you were, I knew he meant it, and was bound to get in touch before very long.'

'That was nearly a month ago.' Kit crossed the hall to

the bedroom. Hugh was taking her to the White Swan, which was a fairly dressy place.

'Your cream jersey silk would be best.' Peg came up behind her. 'It shows off your figure . . . what's left of it! You don't eat enough, you know, Kit. You've lost weight noticeably over the last few months. Do you feel all right?'

'Don't fuss, Peg!' Kit went to the bathroom to shower. She had sidestepped Peg's question, partly because she didn't know how to reply. It was true that for some time now she had felt, not exactly ill, but not exactly well, either; she had swung between the two states in a kind of limbo, that sometimes frightened her. 'You don't mind seeing to Dee, do you?' She stepped under the shower, listening for Peg's reply before she pulled on her cap.

'Don't be daft . . . of course not.' Dee was with Peg now, or rather with Joe, annoying him by stealing his crayons again. If anything should happen to me, Peg would look after Dee, swam hazily and horribly into Kit's mind, as she turned on the taps and soaped herself vigorously . . . there was nothing the matter with her. She was feeling better with every second that passed.

'My new secretary does her job well,' Hugh told her a little later, over smoked salmon and brown bread and butter, in the dining-room of the White Swan.

'I'm glad.'

'But I've missed you and the baby, and I know my housekeeper has.'

'That's a nice thing to say,' said Kit.

'It happens to be true,' he smiled at her over his glass. Their table was set in a bow window that overlooked the river. From where they sat they could see the swans that gave the hotel its name, gliding in and out of the willows, upending now and then, looking haughtily up towards the windows, then more expectantly at the few diners who were eating outside in the still warm sunshine. It was nearly June, the best time of the year.

'Tell me about your work at the General,' said Hugh, when their steaks arrived. 'Don't you find it a little hard going, with your home commitments as well?'

'Perhaps sometimes, yes,' Kit admitted, careful of what she said. She didn't want him to think she regretted her decision to return to ward nursing. 'The General is a very good hospital, and the standard of care is high,' she emphasised, meeting his sandy-lashed eyes.

'I know Professor Planner,' he reached for the pepper-mill. 'You'll have met his team on the ward, I expect, including his new registrar?'

'Mr Niall? Oh, yes, I see him most days.' Kit swallowed a piece of meat rather too soon, and felt it raze her throat.

'I met him socially,' Hugh went on, 'about three weeks ago, when I discovered his father was Max Niall, whom I've known for some little time.'

'Oh, really?' Kit alerted, waiting to hear more.

'He's a dental surgeon, with a practice in Knightsbridge. He also undertakes maxillo-facial surgery at two London clinics. Some years ago I had the misfortune to be mugged outside Harrods. My jaw was injured, and Max Niall was one of the surgeons called in to fix it. After I came out of hospital he attended to my teeth. I was working at Great Ormond Street then; it was when my wife was alive.'

'What a terrible experience . . . how *awful*!' Kit stared at his thin, handsome face.

'It was.' He broke a breadstick, snapping it cleanly like chalk. 'As well as damage to my front teeth I sustained an ugly scar—hence the beard.' He touched it and smiled at her.

'It suits you,' she assured him.

'Yes, it does.' He touched it again.

He wasn't a modest man, Kit recalled, not that she held this against him. He was a successful consultant, and he looked the part, so why shouldn't he be pleased with his eminence and his good looks, and revel in having both? It was towards the end of their main course that he asked her if she would care to go with him to see the play *Carrington's Folly*, which was running at the local theatre during June. 'Does the idea appeal to you, Katherine?' He plainly thought that it would, which made it very embarrassing for her to have to turn him down, but she had to do so because she didn't want to get too involved with him.

'It's a lovely idea, Hugh, and thank you,' she said, 'but I seldom go out in the evenings. It's hardly fair to Peg when she has to look after Dee during the day . . . well, most days, anyway. I'm sure you'll understand.'

'Perfectly.' His reply was prompt, and he quickly thrust the diary he had been pulling out back into his pocket again. It was a difficult moment and Kit felt terrible, for she knew he had taken offence. He began to talk about other things, and she made the right replies, but the awkwardness lodged between them like a rock that wouldn't move. She thought of Tim, she couldn't help it; his reactions had been similar to Hugh's. Tim had hated being refused the tiniest, simplest thing. Were all men like that? Was Charles Niall? Oh, why bring him into it? In any case, the spoken-for Charles would never ask her out. If he did she'd say 'no' and not care a blink how much she offended him. Just for a second a vision of his face, wearing his crinkly smile, hung between her and the sweet trolley, which Hugh waved away, and ordered cheese . . . without consulting her.

It was a relief to both of them, perhaps, when the restaurant manager appeared at their table a few minutes later to summon Hugh to the phone. 'It's the hospital, sir, they said it was urgent!'

Hugh got up at once. 'I'm sorry, Katherine, you'll have to excuse me . . . I hoped this wouldn't happen!' He walked ahead of the manager, out of the room, causing a trail of interest amongst the diners, some of whom stared covertly at Kit. A waiter brought her coffee, and fussed as he poured it out, then the restaurant manager came back in. 'The doctor has had to go,' he informed Kit. 'He asked me to let you know. The bill has been settled and we'll fetch you a taxi, as soon as you want to leave, but please take your time, madam; it's a pleasure to have you here.'

But it wasn't really much of a pleasure to sit there alone. Kit felt conspicuous, and she also felt . . . while realising this was unfair . . . deserted, left high and dry, jettisoned by Hugh. She drank one cup of coffee which she didn't enjoy, then left the restaurant. She fetched her coat—a light cream fun-fur—and stepped out into the night. She didn't want a taxi, it wasn't far to walk, she couldn't *sit* in a taxi; she had to move, to get rid of her feelings . . . what a way to end a birthday! She set off briskly, her high heels clicking, her cream dress and coat making her conspicuous again, as she passed under the lights. There was the bridge to cross, then a short walk down a side road called Castle Close, after that she'd be in the High Street, and only five minutes from home.

A group of youths called out to her as she reached the end of the bridge. They were sitting on the parapet drinking beer; one of them threw a can, not to hit her, but to roll at her feet. Kit side-stepped it and stumbled, then tried to hurry as she righted herself. The youths formed a line behind her, and tailed her as she turned into Castle Close. The noise they made, shouting and jeering, made one of the tenants of Castle Close flats swing round, as he locked his car on the park. It was Charles Niall, and without thinking twice, she bolted through the entrance of the block of flats and ran across to him.

He looked astonished, as well he might; then she felt his hand on her shoulder. 'Kit! Whatever . . .' The boys passed by, still shouting and jeering, and kicking their cans. Charles brought his glance back to her. 'What on earth's going on?' His grip tightened.

'I'm sorry,' she let out her breath, 'I mean, I'm sorry for all the high drama, but I don't especially like being tailed by a bunch of hooligans—I met up with them on the bridge.'

'But what are you doing at this time of night, walking about on your own and dressed . . . and dressed up?' She could see him staring, looking her up and down.

There were enough lights coming from the flats' windows to illuminate the yard. Charles was in slacks and shirt and pullover—the latter had a V-neck; his tie was crooked, and his hair was ruffled; he was frowning and drawing his brows.

'I was having dinner with Hugh,' Kit explained, 'but a phone call took him off . . . there was some sort of emergency . . . we were just at the end of our meal.'

'Of course . . . yes, your mutual birthday! Oh dear, the best laid plans!' He unlocked the car. 'In you get, I'll see you safely home.'

'Mr Niall, you don't have to,' she protested. 'That's not why I charged in here. I looked in and saw you, and came in for . . . well, just for refuge, I think.'

'That was sensible of you, Mrs Tennant. I'm very glad you did.' When he smiled she went weak, her bones turned to water, but she told herself that this was a side-effect of the wine she had drunk, she wasn't used to it. 'I *want* to drive you.' He opened the door, Kit slid in and he closed it. She watched him walking round the car, and then he was in beside her, fastening his seat-belt, switching the engine on.

His nearness was overpowering. She found she couldn't breathe . . . or dared not. The back of her neck went stiff. She tried staring out of the window, but that didn't help overmuch, for on it, reflected in the glass, she could see the shape of Charles's head, and his hands on the wheel, and when he spoke she nearly jumped out of her skin. 'MacBride's registrar is away, you know,' she felt him glance at her. 'Most likely his houseman had orders to call him if anything out of the ordinary turned up, as it so often does, at the most inconvenient times.'

'I'm not blaming Hugh.' And she didn't want to talk about him either.

'There'll be other times.' He stared straight ahead, as they left the High Street behind. They were very nearly home now, here was the left-hand turn into Mount Cliff Road. Was she glad or sorry? A little of both, perhaps.

'Thank you again.' She prepared to get out, as he halted at the kerb.

'I'll see you in.' He got out too, and when they reached the porch he took her key from her and opened the door. 'Good night, then, Kit, sweet dreams.' His hands on her shoulders drew her forward, and she felt the touch of his lips, moth-light, between her brows, then he was off down the path. She watched him till he reached the car, answered his farewell wave, then walked into the hall and relived the scene, all over again. After that she went to check on Dee.

The baby was flat on her back in her cot, arms flung over her head. In eight day's time she would be a year old. While expecting her Kit had thought that she might arrive on her own birthday, the dates lay very close. Peg was laying on a special lunch for them both in the flat tomorrow. Bob didn't work on Saturdays, so the family would be complete. It would be lovely, it was sweet of Peg. Kit tried to think of this and not of Charles, as she drifted off to sleep.

As it happened, though, the family luncheon was never to take place. Shortly after three a.m. she awoke feeling very ill. She had pains in her stomach, all over her abdomen; she groaned and drew up her knees. It was all that rich food—it had to be that, it couldn't be anything else. She rolled out of bed, reached the bathroom and stayed in there some time. She lay on the floor, till the pain seemed to leave her, then it came back, gripping and gnawing. She doubled up and breathed deeply; she would make it, *make* it go. It seemed to lessen . . . it was going . . . it had left her. Lurching to her feet and walking with care in case it should start up all over again, she got through Dee's room into her own, got into bed and lay down. She would have to do something about seeing a doctor, she must make an appointment tomorrow. She had been having too many digestive upsets, she had not felt right for some time. Tomorrow I'll ring and make an appointment . . . I promise, I promise I will. Whom she was promising she had no idea, she was talking to herself, she was spent and exhausted. She closed her eyes and slept.

Light was filtering through the curtains, and the milkman who came at five-thirty was delivering six bottles of milk to the house when Kit next opened her eyes. She opened them, unaware of anything else in the world but pain—a different pain, one that had localised deep in her right groin . . . a worse pain, a leaping agony. She groaned, and doubled up, rocking on the bed; for a second it seemed to stop. She flew to the bathroom, and reached it just as the agony started again, drawing and pulling, jumping like a tooth. She knew what it was—not that that helped. I shall die, I've left it too late. I shall die here with this terrible pain, she thought. It lessened, and she crawled inch by inch by inch by inch . . . over miles and miles of carpet, into the hall, and reached for the telephone. She daren't stand up. She pulled at the flex, and the instrument fell on her. The resultant crash and the cry she gave brought Peg and Bob from the flat—Peg first, a whirling flurry of pale green nightdress, Bob in his dressing-gown, hastily tying the cord.

'Kit darling, whatever . . . oh, Kit!' Peg was on her knees, slipping an arm about her shoulders, helping her sit up. She stared in horror at Kit's grey face, at her sunken dark-ringed eyes. 'Whatever is it . . . why didn't you call?'

'Appendix . . . ambulance . . .' Kit's words were grunts, as another pain leapt and sprang. She was aware of Bob dialling above her, of Peg fetching her duvet and wrapping it round her, her anxious face an inch or two from her own.

Bob had put the door on the latch, and the ambulance-men walked in, complete with stretcher, a few minutes later. 'I can manage . . . to walk as far as . . . the door . . . you don't need . . .' gasped Kit, but she needn't have bothered.

'Easy does it,' they lifted her, 'easy does it, now!' Supine on the stretcher, covered in a blanket, she was carried out of the house, down the steps, down the path and into the ambulance. Bob, who had pulled on slacks and sweater over his striped pyjamas, went with her.

'I'll ring from the hospital,' he told Peg in the porch—a distracted Peg, who had to stay where she was because of the children. The closing of the ambulance doors, the sight of it pulling away, made the shock and fear inside her worsen. She forced herself to control it, by praying hard.

Please let Kit be all right.

CHAPTER SIX

THE NIGHT staff were still on duty when Kit was wheeled into Casualty. Bob supplied all the necessary details, after which she was examined by a tired young doctor, who recognised her at once. 'Who's the surgeon on call?' he asked his nurse. They muttered together outside the cubicle, while Kit, who was feeling to ill to care much about anything, wondered if Charles would be the one to take out her beastly appendix. In an effort to separate mind from body she fixed her eyes on the window that showed the leaves of a plane tree fluttering against the glass. The swish of the cubicle curtains came with a fresh stab of pain, and through it she saw the stocky, bow-fronted shape of the Prof. He was speaking to her, she could see his lips moving; it was like that time in the storm, when she had lip-read Charles's words in the hospital entrance, but now the storm was in her. She was the storm, the whole of it, the storm was taking her over. She knew the Professor was touching her, then the young student nurse was wiping her face and drawing the blanket back up.

'There's not much doubt about that, young lady,' he could hear the Professor now. 'I'm going to have to remove your appendix—you'll have guessed that, I'm sure. Once it's out you'll be all right, no more of that bad pain.' His voice was kind, but his face was high up, dwindling away to a point.

She thought she said 'yes', she must have done so; she knew she signed a form, and then everything happened in quick succession—a succession of preparations which she knew well, knew by heart, and were now happening to her. It was all happening to her now . . . she, Kit

Tennant, was the one going under. 'Will I die?' she asked.

'Not a chance!' She was in the anaesthetic room. The Professor was gloved and ready, looking shorter and wider than ever in his theatre greens and mask. The anaesthetist injected thiopentone into the back of her hand. 'Count up to ten for me, please, Mrs Tennant.' She tried, but after five she drifted off, and after that she knew nothing at all until she came to in the recovery room and saw the white dress of a nurse close beside her, and heard her voice telling her she was fine . . . it was all over and soon she would be in the ward.

'Which . . . ward?' Her mouth felt dry.

'Your own ward, m'dear . . . Bellingham Ward, you'll feel at home there. Couldn't be better, eh?' The Professor was a great one for jokes, though most times they didn't come off. 'It's all over,' he bent to her. 'How are you feeling now?'

'Wonderful!' She smiled at him. 'Oh, wonderful, thank you, sir!' As he bent even lower she kissed him, and put her arm round his neck. It was the effect of the anaesthetic, she was on a kind of high. She felt . . . oh, so grateful, and she said so, and kissed him again. 'Thank you for what you did for me, thank you for what you did. I've always thought you were lovely, and now I know you are.' There were one or two discreet titters, which Kit didn't even hear. She was still reiterating her thanks all the time she was being wheeled out of the recovery room into the lift, and thence to Bellingham Ward. She was asleep again, though, when the lift stopped, and she never really roused all the time Sister Clive and Nurse Geare was getting her settled into the first of the two side-wards, and discussing how they would cope.

'The SNO has promised us a relief nurse,' said Sister. She was sorry Kit was ill, but her mind had to run on practical matters, and the ward was a busy one. She was one nurse short . . . one *good* nurse short. She looked at Kit's sleeping face. Poor kid, she thought, staying behind after Nurse Geare had gone. She looked at the notes that had come up from theatre with Kit. Her appendix had been on the point of rupture. It was lucky that the Prof had been in the building, right on the spot, so no time had been lost. He might be a difficult old boy at times, but his skills were undiminished. Sister left the side-ward, leaving the door ajar.

Miss Jevons, the Senior Nursing Officer, kept to her word. She telephoned the nursing agency and a smiling young staff nurse reported to Sister at twelve-thirty, the start of the second shift. It was she who took in Kit's tea soon after four o'clock. Kit had been awake for some time, and she drank the tea thirstily, leaning back on the bed-rest which the girl had erected for her. 'I'm the relief nurse, taking your place—name of Sheila Barnes,' she told Kit, glancing at her charts.

'Sister will be glad.' Kit's eyes roamed round the smallish room. To think that this time yesterday she had been getting it ready for a new patient, never dreaming who that patient was going to be. And was it really only yesterday? It seemed light years ago. She watched Nurse Barnes being efficient, and wished someone she knew would come in and say 'hello' to her. Did Sister mind her being here? Would the other nurses mind having to look after her? Not that she'd need much nursing; appendicitis, caught in time, was nothing much at all. She moved her legs experimentally, and nothing seemed to hurt. But careful, careful, she told herself . . . try taking a good deep breath. She did so, and immediately felt the protest her abdomen made—a nasty, dragging, pulling feeling, due to her stitches, of course. She placed a tentative hand under her operation gown. She felt the dressing . . . what kind was it? She longed to know more. What she most wanted was to see her notes, but she knew they wouldn't let her—'they' being her nurses, of whom she wasn't one. She was a patient now, she had joined the other side.

Staff Nurse Barnes, smoothing her dress over her plump behind, was on the way out when Charles Niall, accompanied by Sister, walked in, both wearing professional smiles. 'Well, you are a fine one, and no mistake!' said Sister, approaching the bed.

'But sitting up and taking notice.' Charles was already turning to the treatment sheet in the brand-new folder of notes.

'And wanting to know all about herself, down to the last stitch, if I read her face aright.' Sister's smile deepened in warmth.

Seeing it, Kit felt relief. So she doesn't mind, she thought, so it *is* all right, I *am* welcome, but I still feel one hell of a nuisance. She looked at her cup, weak tears filling her eyes.

Charles scraped a chair across the floor, then sat down facing the bed. He sat bolt upright, long legs crossed, white coat falling apart. Didn't he ever button it up? Perhaps he couldn't be bothered, or hadn't time, or liked it as it was. His trousers were impeccable, so was his shirt. Kit's eyes travelled upwards and remained on his face, as he gave her the clinical details she wanted. 'The Professor used a transverse incision,' he told her. 'It should heal very quickly, leaving no weakness.' He glanced down at the notes.

'Oh, good,' said Kit, feeling pleased, for a bikini cut was the best. It was easily hidden, so she wouldn't look battle-scarred when she spread herself out on the shingle beach at Barhampton at weekends.

'By this time next week, if the Professor agrees, your stitches will come out, after which I expect he'll discharge you, and that will be that!' Charles smiled at her and closed the folder of notes.

'When will I be able to come back to work?' Her green-hazel eyes didn't waver from his; her hair hung limp, her face was colourless. She made an unwary movement and winced as her stitches dragged.

'The Professor will no doubt leave that in abeyance,' Charles said consolingly. Sister had slipped out of the room to speak to June Stenson's mother.

'It's visiting time, isn't it?' Kit was trying to sort herself out. 'It's so strange being a patient.' She watched Charles get to his feet. 'It's like looking through the same window, but from the other side.'

'Like *Through the Looking-Glass*, perhaps.' He could see that she was tired; her eyes were closing, and he took the cup from her hand. Their fingers touched, but it was comfort this time that spread from him to her, making her feel secure and . . . secure and . . . marvellous. She drifted off and in seconds was asleep.

Peg came during evening visiting, which was three hours later. She brought flowers, toiletries, glucose sweets; she changed Kit from her hospital gown into one of her pretty nighties, and helped her brush her hair. 'Sister said I could, so don't worry,' she told her.

'I'm not,' smiled Kit, 'but it does seem strange to be waited on hand and foot like this. All the nurses have been in to say "hello", and I've been out of bed.'

'Already?' Peg looked scandalised.

'Yes, and tomorrow, with any luck, I shall stagger along to the bathrooms.' She took one of the glucose sweets and sucked it with enjoyment. It wasn't so bad, being an invalid.

Peg was wearing a fluffy cardigan, and she unbuttoned it at the neck. 'I can't tell you how ghastly I felt,' she said, 'when you went off in the ambulance. I know you said it was appendicitis, but I couldn't help wondering if you were going to come through it all . . . you looked so dreadfully ill.'

'Well, I have—I've sailed through. I had ace attention . . . the Professor himself. It seems he slept in the building that night, so he was on the premises. If he hadn't been, I suppose Charles Niall would have operated.' A frisson of pure embarrassment swept Kit, as she thought how simply terrible that would have been . . . not at the time, but facing him afterwards. 'And how's my darling Dee?' she asked Peg, who reassured her at once.

'She's in bouncing form . . . literally! We've moved her cot upstairs; it's easier, and she loves being in with Joe. She misses you, though, I can tell she does.' Peg was ever tactful. She knew Kit wouldn't want to think that Dee could do without her. And when you were ill you felt things like that more. 'I don't suppose you'll be in here long, I expect you'll soon be home?'

'In a week or ten days, with any luck. Oh yes, and that reminds me . . . I don't want Mother and Dad told, Peg; they'll only be upset. They'll come tearing down all the way from Scotland, and there's no need for that. I'll write to them when I get home. I don't want them worried now.'

'Well, all right, if you're sure . . .'

'I *am* sure.' But why was Peg looking so fussed? 'What's on your mind? I can tell something is!' Kit felt fagged out again. It was amazing how even a little thing like a simple appendicectomy could make one feel so droopy, after only a few minutes' chat. She could actually feel her eyes closing, as though she had weights on her lids. But then when she heard what Peg was saying, she was jerked back to wakefulness. Her mother-in-law, Harriet Tennant, was coming to stay.

'She rang up early this morning,' said Peg, 'to know about the parcel—whether you'd got it safely, and did Dee like her toy? She naturally expected to speak to you, so what could I do but tell her? I had to, Kit, and it was all I could do to stop her coming *then*. In the end she agreed to hold her horses until the day before you're discharged, then she'll come and stay till you're strong again, to look after you and Dee. I couldn't do anything about it—you know what Harriet's like.'

'Domineering, overwhelming, kind and devoted to Dee,' Kit said, leaning back on her pillows, and trying not to mind. She didn't want Harriet, and she knew she didn't; the thought of her booming voice, and her energy, and all her advice, was weakening to say the least. But on the other hand she was Tim's mother, Dee was her only grandchild, the only one she would ever have, and she loved coming to stay. Her husband was a newspaper correspondent, and was often abroad for long stretches. 'Yes, she'll have to come, Peg. She means well. I dare say I'll survive. Now don't give me any more shocks like that or my temperature will rise!' They giggled together, then talked about other things.

But later, when Peg had gone home, the thought occurred to Kit that Harriet's coming would tend to make life easier for her cousin. Peg had quite enough to do without having to lend a hand to a semi-invalid who might not be able to lift her baby about, or plug in a vacuum cleaner, or wash and iron, or shop . . . or not very much, not for a week or so. Harriet would take all that in her stride as well as jog before breakfast. So by the time the night staff had come on duty, and the smell of heating milk was wafting across the corridor into side ward one, Kit had managed to convince herself that her mother-in-law's visit would be a godsend. And after that she slept.

She was out of bed for a short time next morning, and had no sooner climbed back in then the hospital chaplain came to see her before going into the day-room for the Sunday service which he always conducted at ten. 'Well, your role has been reversed, Staff Nurse!' The chaplain was a small, sprightly oval-shaped man, his domed and balding head accentuating his likeness to a pale brown egg. He beamed at Kit, asked how she was feeling, then went off before she could answer. He had to get the service in before his ordinary church one. He was running very late this morning, and it was necessary to rush the hymns and prayers through at top speed, which he very much deplored. The last hymn—'New every Morning'—was a favourite of Kit's. She could hear the patients singing it, and she especially liked the words: 'Through sleep and darkness safely brought, restored to life, and power, and thought.' And that, she felt, summed up her own case exactly. The dark, worrying shadow that had been dogging her for weeks had been dealt with and cast away; she was going to be all right. She couldn't help smiling, her face just did it without any help from her; she was still smiling when Dick Parker, accompanied by Sheila Barnes, the relief nurse, put his head round the door.

'Now this is what you might call a turn-up for the book! Do you mean to tell me you've changed sides, gone over to the patients!'

'Looks like it. Sorry, Dick, for adding to your troubles.'

'You had a rough time for a few hours, I hear.' He unclipped her charts from the bed.

'You can say that again!' Kit exclaimed with feeling. 'It was worse than when I had Dee . . . at least that was productive.'

'Yes, I see what you mean.' Dick had a look at her abdomen without disturbing the dressing. 'How does it feel?'

'Draggy, but otherwise all right.' She stared down at the line of Elastoplast, which she knew lay over a dressing, probably sealed with Nobecutane, which she knew the Professor favoured.

'There's no sign of peripheral inflammation,' said Dick, as Nurse Barnes covered her up. 'The dressing won't need to be disturbed till your stitches are removed. Charles Niall is off duty, by the way, so you won't be bothered with any more of the Prof's team . . .

not on the Sabbath day!' He went off grinning, and Nurse Barnes followed him out.

Dick was wrong, as it happened, for Charles, who had lunched near the hospital, decided to call in and see two patients—one of them being Kit. He came, not in a professional capacity, but as an ordinary visitor, arriving on Bellingham Ward just after two. He was formally dressed in a dark lounge suit, with a rather splendid tie of blue and grey stripes, which hung straight down for once.

Kit, awakening from a light doze, found him sitting by her bed. 'Mr Niall!' she exclaimed. She remembered not to jerk up too quickly and, more importantly, remembered not to call him 'Charles' as she often did in her thoughts.

'You're looking much better.' He had laid a sheaf of carnations on her locker.

'Are those from you? Oh, they're lovely—thank you!' She was charmed, she could hardly believe it . . . flowers from him! She lifted them up and buried her face in their scent. 'I *feel* better,' she said quickly, feeling suddenly shy of him. 'I just get a jab when I move sometimes, but I'm learning by degrees.'

'I hope you've been up and walking about.' His tone was brusque again. 'Bed is a dangerous place after surgery, as I'm sure you know only too well.'

'I *do* know, and I *have* been up—not into the day-room as yet, but I've been across the corridor, and walking about in here.'

'I'm glad to hear it,' he relented, and smiled. 'And I shouldn't be preaching at you, because this is a friendly visit, not a professional call.'

'Oh.' This threw her for a second or two; she sniffed at her flowers again.

'Yes, I've been having lunch with the Professor at his house in Challoners Way. Being so near it seemed a good plan to call in here to see a young lad I know in

Kilross, and also to look in on you.'

'Nice of you.' Kit's smile felt forced, but she kept it pinned in place. It didn't escape her notice that Charles was taking infinite pains to let her know that she wasn't the sole reason for his coming to the General Hospital on a Sunday afternoon.

'I told the Professor I was coming, and he sent his regards. I expect you'll be seeing him on Tuesday, or he'll see you . . . there's to be a teaching round, I believe.'

'Oh well, I'll survive, I suppose.' She didn't exactly relish being ringed by medics, but there it was, they all had to learn. 'I'll be glad to see the Professor,' she told Charles, 'to thank him for everything.'

'I understand that you *have* thanked him, very handsomely . . . at least, that's what he told me, over lunch today.' Charles was smiling . . . no, grinning. Kit felt herself grow warm.

'What do you mean?' she jerked out, just as Sister looked in at the door. Charles spoke to her, said something about not being very long. Kit heard their exchange of words in a buzz about her ears. Whatever had he meant by her thanking the Professor, and why had he laughed like that? Surely she hadn't made an ass of herself when she'd surfaced from the anaesthetic. Patients sometimes did, she knew that; they said and did very strange things.

'Do you mean I thanked him in the recovery room?' she asked, when Sister had gone.

'More than that . . . you sat up and embraced him, and called him a lovely man!'

'Oh, no!' she gasped.

'Oh, yes! And what's more he liked it, it made him grow half a foot taller.'

Kit flushed scarlet. 'He must have known it wasn't really me talking. He shouldn't have told you.'

'I think he was boasting,' said Charles, 'and I can't say

that I blame him. I just felt he was lucky to be on the receiving end. I wouldn't have minded those kind of thanks, nor being told I was lovely. Don't worry about it,' he took her hand and gave it a gentle squeeze. 'We all need praise at times, even anaesthetic-induced!'

'Even you?'

'Especially me.' He released her hand as he spoke. His mouth still smiled, but his eyes went bleak. 'I think I should go,' he said. 'You'll be having other visitors, they're probably waiting now.' No sooner had he spoken than the door opened to admit Sister again, followed this time by Hugh MacBride, who was carrying high in his arms a baby girl in a yellow smocked dress, who gave a loud KERRrrr of delight when she saw her mother, and made pat-a-cake claps with her hands.

'*Dee*! Oh, Dee!' was all Kit could say. She held out her arms for her daughter.

'I knew you'd want to see her.' Hugh passed the baby over. Kit hugged her tightly. It was almost too much; she shed tears, but only Dee saw. How wonderful to have her, to touch her, to hold her. She felt so grateful to Hugh. Dee showed her pleasure by butting her head against her mother's hair, and trying to touch her teeth when Kit smiled at her.

Charles Niall and Hugh MacBride were renewing their acquaintance, exchanging the kind of banalities that near-strangers do, when they meet again unexpectedly. Sister, after a last look at Dee, went back into her office. Charles spoke to the baby, but kept his distance, as he made his way to the door. 'I was just saying it was time I was off. Good to see you again, MacBride.' He looked at Kit holding her child. 'Keep up the fine start you've made.'

'I intend to,' she said. 'I need to be well for the best possible reasons.' Her chin ruffled the baby's hair, her smile was radiant; it encompassed Hugh, who was standing by the bed. With a last glance in their direction,

Charles nodded goodbye, then went out and closed the door.

Hugh seated himself on the vacant chair, unbuttoning the jacket of his dove grey suit. He turned his head to Kit. 'How are you feeling?'

'Absolutely fine.'

'I'm glad to hear it,' he said. He took Dee from her and set her down on the floor. Immediately she started her exploring tactics, and they couldn't help laughing at her, as she crawled away, moving sideways like a crab.

Kit asked him how he had heard about her sudden admission to hospital. 'From Robert Farthingdale—you know, my registrar. His wife had a baby son last night, here at the General; Rob was in at the birth. He was coming down from Maternity Block, and saw you brought into Cas. I saw him at St Margaret's this morning and he told me all about it. I rang your cousin, and she filled me in with the rest.'

'They were very quick once I got here,' Kit told him. 'I had spot-on treatment. I ought to be discharged after next weekend.'

'That's splendid . . . a good job over.' Hugh looked at her quizzically. 'But didn't you have any warning at all that something might be amiss? I ask because I couldn't help noticing, when we met on Friday, that you'd lost weight; you looked fine-drawn. Now that leads me to think . . .'

'Yes, all right, I confess!' She bit her lip. 'I'd been having one or two symptoms . . . dyspepsia, that sort of thing.'

'But surely you saw your GP?'

'No.'

'Then you were very unwise. You must have known how risky it was to let symptoms of that kind ride. Supposing it had been Delia, you would have called in a doctor double-quick, now wouldn't you?' He raised his chin in query—a chin made longer by the incidence of his beard.

'Yes, I would,' she admitted readily, but impatiently too, for he must have known how different the two issues were. Hugh was an expert on child care, but he had a lot to learn about human nature in general and women in particular. In a bid to try to get him away from the subject of her illness, she asked him how he had managed to cope with Dee in his car. 'Did you get her baby-seat out of my Metro?' she asked.

'No, I didn't need to,' he said, 'Mrs Carlton sat in the rear and held Dee on her lap. Joe sat with her, thrilled, incidentally, to be coming in to see you. Mr Carlton sat in the front with me.'

'You mean, in your car?'

'I mean in the Jag. It seemed to me to be best. I shall take them home, naturally; get myself some tea, while they're in here with you. I'm glad I came,' Hugh added pointedly.

Kit felt less than gracious. What was she thinking about? She hadn't given him much of a welcome, just made a fuss of Dee, forgetting who it was who had brought her . . . *and* her family as well.

'Oh, Hugh, I couldn't be more glad!' And now she felt she was gushing. 'You've been so kind,' she went on more quietly, 'and spared so much of your time coming from Cawnford and all the way out to Hilldown.'

'I had the time to spare, as it happened.' He was scooping Dee off the floor. 'I'll go out now, let the others come in.' He handed the baby to Kit. 'If I can I'll come in later in the week, it depends on how things go.' He was being cautious, he hadn't forgiven her for refusing his theatre invitation. But of course, she hadn't been well on Friday . . . not her usual self. That might account for a very great deal; he began to feel better at once, especially when she told him, sounding as though she meant it, that she would be glad to see him when he wasn't too busy to come.

Peg couldn't praise him enough. 'He thinks such a lot of you, Kit. When we said we were coming in to see you, he wanted to be involved. I thought he intended to meet us here, but just after lunch he bowled up in that gorgeous car, and suggested we all rode in that. Do you think I ought to ask him to tea, after we get back home?'

'He's having tea here,' Kit told her. How Peg went on at times. She turned to Joe, who was all agog to know if her tummy hurt, and was it sewn up, and could he see it, please?

'It's a little sore, and yes, it's sewn up, and no, you can't see it, Joe.' She gave him a sweet, which stopped his chatter, allowing his father to tell her about a piano recital he had heard on Radio Three.

Bob was still shaken by Kit's illness. He was very fond of her. Like Peg, he hoped she would marry again, but he very much wished that his wife hadn't earmarked MacBride for her, which he happened to know she had. He didn't believe in trying to matchmake, he thought that the Boy with the Arrow did a better job, if left to judge for himself.

Being a patient, as Kit discovered over the next eight days, wasn't really all that bad, but then, as she told herself, she wasn't a desperately ill patient, and hadn't a lot to bear. She could get up and wash herself, she could read to her heart's content, the meals were OK—similar to those served in the canteen upstairs—and going through into the day-room to exchange news and views with other patients had its amusing side. June Stenson was the only one of the old consignment left; the others were all fairly new admittances who had never met Kit as a nurse. June never mixed with anyone, she only appeared in the day-room if driven there by Sister; she preferred to sit by her bed, or wander up and down the corridor, peering into the rooms. On the Thursday, much to Kit's surprise, she came into her room shortly after breakfast, as Kit was reading the paper.

'Why, hello, June,' she said, 'come and keep me company . . . use that chair, if you like. How are you feeling?' She laid her newspaper down.

'I'm all right, going home at the weekend.' June, in a Mickey Mouse nightshirt that reached to her knees, perched on the chair near Kit's bcd.

'Oh well, you'll beat me, then. I *hope* to be discharged on Monday,' said Kit. 'It's my small daughter's birthday tomorrow and I would like to have been out for that.'

June shrugged. She didn't appear to be interested. 'I don't suppose,' she said, 'that I'll be able to enter for the show-jumping this year, at the County Show in July. I don't suppose you've ever been to it,' she added scornfully.

'If you mean the Bewlis Agricultural Show, yes, I have, as a matter of fact. I went last year and had a great time,' Kit fell silent, remembering it. Harriet, her mother-in-law, had been staying at Hilldown, Dee had been a month old. It had been Kit's first outing since her birth. She had gone to the Bewlis Show with Peg and Bob.

'Are you going this year?' she heard June ask.

'I'd not really thought about it . . . possibly, yes,' Kit considered the matter, 'but I may be back here working by then.'

'Sooner you than me,' sniffed June, getting up to go. 'I don't know how you stick this place.' Giving her nightshirt a jerk, she took herself off, looking about twelve years old.

Kit stared at the door which June had slammed. What a solitary girl she was. Her parents visited regularly, but she appeared to have very few friends. On the whole that wasn't surprising, but a pity, all the same. Kit thought of her own stream of visitors, of the nurses' friendliness, of Sister coming in to chat, not to mention the ward domestics, and the Chaplain, and the lady who brought the library books. Then there was the family, of course . . . Peg and Bob and the children. Tomorrow there would be Harriet Tennant, her mother-in-law, as well. Charles had never come again, not as a visitor. When he stepped inside her room it was simply and solely in his role as the Professor's assistant. Dick came in most days.

Hugh came to suit his work schedule. Sister always let him in. 'He's such a charming man, I always think,' she said to Kit one day. 'I wonder if he ever feels he would like to go back up north. He comes from my part of the world, you know; he's an Edinburgh man. The South is all right in its way, but . . .' her eyes had gone to the window where, possibly, instead of the Downs she saw the lowlands of Scotland, and a different castle, and the grandeur of Princes Street. 'Still, here I am, and likely to stay.' Sister Clive was thirty-two. It would take some persuasion to shift her from Bewlis in East Sussex, where she had a small house and a friend to share it with.

The Professor, flanked by Sister and Dick, had seen Kit yesterday, making the welcome decision that her stitches could come out today. She could then be discharged on Monday, when Dick had seen her again. And right now, judging from the sounds coming from outside her door, Sister and Jean Holden were about to make their way in, with a dressings trolley. Stitch-drawing time was here!

'I've seldom seen a neater scar,' said Sister a few minutes later, flicking the last of the nylon sutures into the receiver, and telling Jean to cover the area with gauze and elastoplast . . .' just to stop any rub, it's bound to feel tender at first.'

'It feels good to me.' Kit got out of bed and reached for her dressing-gown. Later, feeling in need of company, she helped Rosa and Marylyn with the mid-morning drinks, and she had her own coffee with them. 'I'm perfectly fit to go home *now*,' she told

Charles that afternoon. He had come up to do a whistle-stop ward round before the start of his holiday. He was going to Cornwall for three weeks, he told Sister, when she enquired. Kit sat at the side of her bed and listened, watching him write in her notes. She reiterated her wish to be discharged.

'Well now, you can have your way. The Prof says you can go home tomorrow. You've made wonderful progress—shows you've a strong constitution.' He handed the notes to Dick.

'I've had good care,' Kit told him.

'She's been a good patient,' Sister put in loyally.

'And I hope,' said Kit, looking at Charles who stood at the foot of the bed, 'that you have an enjoyable holiday.' The stiffly formal words seemed to clog her throat. He was going away, but then, in a sense, so was she, for she wouldn't be back at the hospital, not in a working capacity, for another month, and at home she was less likely to think about him. At least she wouldn't be watching the door, which Sister was now opening, wondering if and when he might come in.

'I hope to get in some surfing,' he was saying cheerfully. 'Fistral Beach at Newquay is pretty well perfect for that. The Atlantic Ocean has the edge on the Channel for exhilarating sports.'

He went out in a breezy fashion, practically rubbing his hands. He was dying to start his leave; he couldn't wait to get free of the hospital, and everyone in it.

And who could blame him for that?

CHAPTER SEVEN

DURING the week of the annual Agricultural Show the town of Bewlis changed its face. It acquired a glitter, a festive air, it was very much en fête. Posters were pasted to bus shelters, listing the events; the High Street was awash with flags, and all along the route that led to the Show were strung-out banners advertising fodder, and sheep dips, and vaccines, and farm machinery. Exhibitors came from near and far, many of them knowing one another, which tended to make this very important date on the calendar a social one as well as a trade event.

Kit, who had been out of hospital exactly a month, took Joe to the Show on the afternoon of Saturday, the last day. He wanted to see the cattle and the horses, visit the small funfair, and have a ride on the children's roundabout. Joe was a little down in the dumps and he needed a treat of some kind. Yesterday his parents had gone off to Bourton in the Cotswolds. It was their sixth wedding anniversary, and this was the first time they had been back to the small hotel where they had spent their honeymoon. Harriet Tennant and Kit were only too glad to look after Joe, so there was no reason why Peg and Bob shouldn't steal two days on their own. Joe had pulled a long face and cried . . . why couldn't he go too? . . . but he had cheered up when Kit suggested the Show.

They went by bus; Kit felt she couldn't cope with the car parking difficulties. They travelled on top, which was Joe's choice, he liked to see about. He was going to be a bus driver when he grew up, he told Kit, and he wouldn't be nasty to anyone, not like their driver today, who had shouted at the old man who caught his stick in the door.

Kit smiled and let Joe chatter on. She was busy with her own thoughts, which ran back over the past few weeks of semi-convalescence. Harriet had been wonderful, there was no doubt about that. The flat had been spring-cleaned, the garden manicured, the washing-machine had never stopped spinning, while delicious and nourishing meals were served up three times a day, with milky snacks in between. Dee had been made far too much of, but Kit tried to turn a blind eye. Harriet wouldn't be with them for ever, and Dee *was* her grandchild. It was best to say nothing, and hope that no harm would be done.

Harriet never appeared to flag. When Kit got out of bed at seven-thirty each morning and drew the curtains back, there would be her mother-in-law in track-suit and trainers, returning from her jog to the Castle. She did it in rain or shine, or gale force wind. 'I never catch chills,' she said. 'She was going home to Kent tomorrow, as her husband Alan would be back from his special assignment in Nicaragua.

Hugh had come to Hilldown twice, and once he had taken Kit to his house at Cawnford to see the changes he had made to some of the rooms. He thoroughly approved of Harriet. 'Her heart's in the right place,' he said. With this Kit agreed, but she couldn't help wondering what Hugh would have said if he knew that her mother-in-law considered him vain and puffed up. 'He only seems to be like that, he's different when you know him,' defended Kit, deploring the fact that Harriet had a habit of running her friends down whenever they came to the house. She was possessive, but still, not to worry, she was going home tomorrow. Kit's spirits began to lift.

On attending Outpatients a week ago, she had been told by the Professor, who was taking the clinic in Charles's absence, that she was doing very well. 'In another month from now, Staff Nurse, you can take up your duties again.'

She had stared at him, for he had to be joking. 'I don't need another month! I'm fit now, I can start now, I hoped you would say next week.'

'I'm afraid not,' the Prof had been obdurate. 'We don't want to rush things, you know, or as my good father would have said, we don't want to spoil the ship for a ha'porth of tar!' He had laughed at his little joke. Kit wasn't amused and she didn't laugh, unlike Dick Parker, who felt he had to. Kit had felt helpless and cross.

Charles would have signed me off, she thought, as the bus gathered speed. They were out of the High Street, which made things easier, but not for very long. As soon as they got within sight of the showground, it was bumper-to-bumper and stop-and-start-and-jerk all over again. 'We could have walked more quickly, couldn't we, Joe?' she smiled at the little boy.

'Yes, and beat the bus,' he said, with his nose glued to the window. He was watching out for the house that had got gnomes in its front garden. He had seen it before when his father had brought him to the park. There were hundreds and hundreds of gnomes, and the house was called Gnome Cottage. There it was, he could see it now . . . his nose was a whitened blob as he stared, and breathed and made mist on the windowpane.

The band was playing *Colonel Bogey* as Kit and Joe, having clambered down from the top of the bus and crossed the busy road, pushed through the turnstiles into the showground, and stood still for a few seconds taking in the scene that met their eyes. Normally the park was just a park, with trees and grass and seats, and the bandstand, of course, but the Show had changed all that. The whole area, which stretched right over to Bewlis racecourse, was a welter of stalls and tents and marquees and rearing farm machinery. Flags fluttered, awnings flapped, while the bleats and blares and grunts of farm animals mingled strangely with the buzz of human voices, as more and more people pushed their way into the grounds.

Kit looked around her, shading her eyes. Where should they make for first? Hugh was meeting them later on, so perhaps if they went to the tea tent she could buy an ice for Joe and study the plan in the catalogue; the tea tent was just in front of them.

Fifteen minutes later, with Joe still spooning ice-cream, Kit, having worked out their plan of campaign till the time came for meeting Hugh, sat watching the tide of people flowing into the tent. So many people, so many faces, yet not one that I know, drifted through her mind at the self-same second that she saw Charles Niall in the midst of the crowd, within a few yards of her. He looked tanned and fit, casually dressed in jeans and an open-necked shirt. He was engaged in conversation with an older man at his side. Kit watched them, with fast-beating heart, her mouth going dry as dust. The older man might be his father, their looks were similar. They were going towards the long trestle tables where tea was being poured out. She could still see them, see their heads. Now they were coming back, each with a cup of tea held high, looking round for seats. Any minute, any second, Charles was going to see her. She tensed herself for his greeting, then relaxed as, once again, they turned their backs. They had found seats at a table some distance away.

Kit let out her breath and moistened her lips; she hadn't seen Charles for a month. It seemed as though his three weeks in Cornwall with the trendy Faith Melville had done him good. Why, even the back of his head had a satisfied look. She had found out by chance, really, that Faith had been there as well. A fortnight ago, while passing the Craft Shop, she had had a good look inside it. She had seen, not Faith, but a blond young man in velvet trousers and smock. She asked Bob that evening if Faith had engaged an assistant. 'More of a locum,' said Bob.

'He's there while Faith's in Newquay, at her other shop, she'll be back at the end of June.'

The dates coincided with Charles's absence; he had mentioned surfing in Newquay. It didn't take much to work out the rest. Good luck to them, Kit had thought. But thought and feeling don't always match up, and what she felt was unhappy, at least for a time, but in the end, after much self-counselling, she got her emotions under proper control again. After all, as she reminded herself, up until her illness she hadn't liked Charles very much, even though the sight of him brought alive sensations she had always tried to ignore. The fact that she now liked him rather more made a weak link in the chain of her armour against him, but so long as she knew it, she could strengthen it again. She would not be made miserable by thinking of him and Faith in Cornwall together. She would think of them and feel nothing at all, she would simply come to terms with the situation, and get on with her life. It was alarming, therefore, having made this firm and sensible resolution, to feel sliced in two when she spotted Charles in the tent.

Joe had finished his ice cream, but he still had the wafer to eat. It was a fan-shaped, fluted wafer, and he nibbled it round the edge. He was so absorbed that he didn't notice anyone stop at his table, not until Aunt Kit said. 'Joe, you remember Mr Niall.' He looked up to see two men there. One of them left very soon, but the one he had met before sat down and told Aunt Kit that his father always came to Bewlis for the Show.

'He's been with me since the weekend, actually.' Charles cast an eye over Kit. She had filled out a little, she was lightly tanned, and her long green eyes met his gaze under her fringe of new-penny hair. 'You look well,' he remarked.

'I am well, which is why it's so ridiculous that I can't go back on duty. I'm ready to go back and, as you know, I only work part-time.' She emphasised the last three words, realising, as she did so, that the thrust was a cheap one; she felt ashamed of herself.

'Even part-time would be too much at present.' He didn't rise to the bait. He probably didn't even see it. Kit struggled between relief and mild frustration . . . did nothing get under his skin?

'My nursing book says that full manual work can be re-started four weeks after a simple appendicectomy,' she said defensively. 'Mine was simple, I had no complications, so I can't see the point of spending another three weeks at home on the sick list.'

'I sympathise,' Charles leaned towards her, resting his arms on the table, 'but I couldn't go against the Prof, you know, even if I wanted to, which I don't in this case; you can do with the extra time.'

'I'm needed on the ward.' But *was* she? she wondered. Nurse Barnes, the agency girl, was filling in most capably. Dick had told her that.

'No one is indispensable.' Charles's remark, coming then, was a shade unfortunate, and Kit but her lip against an angry retort. 'Can't you go away for a while,' he suggested, 'visit your parents, perhaps?'

'They live in Scotland, they're both working, and it's too far to go. I wouldn't want to take Dee all that way, and Mother and Dad are coming to Bewlis anyway, during the late summer.'

'My parents both work.' Charles changed tack a little. 'Father's a dental surgeon, Mother's a gynaecologist. There are times when I think they work far harder than I do. At least I've had a break.'

'Did you enjoy it?' She met his eyes.

'Very much,' he said smoothly. 'At the risk of sounding old hat, it was just what the doctor ordered.'

Faith and he together in Cornwall, Faith and he making love. Kit felt uncomfortable. She looked away, she tried to say something apt. Then Joe, who was getting extremely bored, chipped in with the remark that they were meeting Dr MacBride at five, and wasn't it time to go.

'It's not four yet, Joe.' Kit wiped his mouth and gave his shorts a hitch. 'Hugh's meeting us at the Highland cattle enclosure at five o'clock,' she said, looking across at Charles who was getting to his feet.

'A fitting place to meet a Scotsman.' He lifted his chair away from the table, then placed it underneath. 'As for me, I'd better join my father in the depths of the flower marquee.' He walked with them to the tent exit, then left them there in the sunshine, with joking admonishments not to get lost.

'Where's he going?' asked Joe, in the way that children have when they don't especially want an answer; he skipped along at Kit's side. They were going to see the Shetland ponies, and the donkeys and the goats. He might have a ride on a donkey, perhaps, or even on a pony. He did, he had both, and he also spent a long time at the funfair. Kit got quite dizzy watching him whirl by on the children's roundabout. Getting him off it for the very last time, she walked with him to the part of the grounds that had been set out as a small covered market. Joe lagged and dragged at Kit's hand. 'We must buy a present for Aunt Harriet,' she said, as they stopped at a stall selling homemade perfumes and herbs and natural medicines. Standing Joe in front of her, where he could see, she examined several articles, trying to decide between a herbal pillow and a shallow bowl of potpourri. Taking the advice of the girl in charge, she opted for the pillow. It was expensive, but if Harriet liked it that was all that mattered.

Swinging her shoulder bag round to the front, she made to unzip it . . . but she never did. Instead she froze, staring at the spot where Joe should have been standing right in front of her feet. He wasn't there . . . *he wasn't there*! She wheeled round, calling his name, she looked to the right and left of her. 'Joe, where are you . . . come here!' Nothing happened, the child didn't come, there was just the press of people all about her, trying to get to the stall. She pushed through them, searching and calling, while alarm mounted to fear. She ran back to the stall and spoke to the girl. 'Did you see the little boy who was with me here? Did you see him go . . . did you see which way he went?'

'I saw him, yes, standing right here,' the girl, who had green fingernails, pointed to the edge of the stall, 'but I didn't see him go. Gone off, has he? That's kids for you, but he can't have got very far.' From her elevated position on a form behind the stall, she scanned the crowd. 'Can't see him, sorry!' She turned to serve the next customer.

As for Kit, she plunged back into the crowd and fought her way out to the pathway. Here there was room to move more easily, but still no sign of Joe. People were passing and repassing; she appealed to one or two: 'Have you seen a little boy in red shorts?' . . . 'Have you seen a little boy?' . . . 'Have you seen a little boy on his own, a little boy with fair hair?' . . . 'Have you seen . . . have you seen . . . have you seen a little boy . . . he was with me, now he's gone!' She was panicking, and she knew she was, she must stop it, stop it at once. She must stop and think, she must make herself think and reason out where he might be. Could he have found his way back to the funfair? She thought he might have done. Yes, yes, that was where he would be. He hadn't wanted to leave there. She would go there first . . . she would go there at once. She prayed as she ran, prayed and hoped as she threaded her way through to the edge of the funfair, to the Jack and Jill chute, to the blaring roundabout. She went straight to the latter, straight to the man dressed like Postman Pat, who was taking the money, and grabbed him by the arm. 'Please, have you seen the little boy who was here a few minutes ago, he was here with me, he was wearing red shorts; he went on the roundabout.'

'Yes, I remember him, love.' He scratched the back of his neck. 'What's happened, then? Strayed, has he? I've not seen him come back here. There's a lost children's hut over there, by the Spillers' advertisement.' He pointed a uniformed arm over the head of a little girl who was mounting the roundabout steps. 'Hope you manage to find him,' he added, leaving Kit to stand in a haze of indecision at first, before making her way to the donkeys and Shetland ponies. Joe might, just might be there. She shrank from reporting him lost, for he wasn't . . . he wasn't actually lost. He must be nearby, he *couldn't* have got very far.

There were several children making friends with the ponies, there were one or two astride donkeys, watched by parents, or nannies, or au pairs, or responsible guardians. But Joe wasn't amongst them, and he hadn't been seen. 'Not since you brought him here just before four,' the girl in jodhpurs said. 'If I were you I'd go to the lost children's hut. They'll give out over their microphone that the little boy is missing. Someone's bound to spot him and take him there. It's the best thing to do. You can search for everlasting, you know, in crowds like these.'

She'll be talking about needles in haystacks soon! Kit thought hysterically, how fitting for an agricultural show—then she made herself calm down. She had got to report Joe missing; she had simply got to do it. Dear God, he was lost! She began to run over the grass.

She was breathless by the time she got to the hut, which was like a small bungalow. She gasped out her message, staring distractedly at two tiny tots playing with a horse and waggon on the floor. 'They're not lost, they're mine,' the official in charge told her. 'Now, don't worry, Mrs Tennant, Joe will be found, someone will bring him here. I'll make an announcement over the microphone now. I shall repeat it every ten minutes until the child appears. Now sit down and wait, it's all you can do. My wife will make you some tea.'

'I couldn't drink it, please don't bother.' Kit didn't feel her throat would widen enough to let anything through it; she found herself wringing her hands. Where was Joe? Where could he be? Somewhere out there in those crowds—crowds of all sorts of people too. She sickened and closed her eyes. It was at this point exactly, as though to worsen her fears, that a police message was given out from the mobile van next door.

'Attention please . . . attention please . . . this is a police message. We have to warn you that thieves are at work in the grounds. Please guard your possessions, take special care in the marquees. Thank you, ladies and gentlemen . . . enjoy your afternoon.'

'Well, now that he's got that off his chest, we'll relay our own bulletin,' the official said smilingly, putting a hand on Kit's shoulder. He wasn't blind to her chalk-white face, neither was his wife. They exchanged glances over her head, and the woman sat with her while the message about Joe was given out.

'This is a call from the lost children's crêche, from the lost children's crêche. Will anyone seeing a little boy of five walking about on his own please bring him here to the crêche where his aunt is waiting for him. He has fair hair, he's wearing red shorts and a white T-shirt, his name is Joe Carlton. Please bring Joe to the children's crêche where his aunt is waiting for him.'

'I can't believe this is happening,' Kit whispered through frozen lips. 'I can't believe it . . . it's like a nightmare!' She jerked to her feet and stared out at the sea of people from the ramp of the bungalow-hut. Joe was there somewhere, he was out there somewhere. 'I shall have to go and look. I can't just stand here doing nothing . . . I shall have to go and look!' She was telling the kindly official this, just as a tall figure filled the doorway, and she turned slowly round to see Charles standing there. For one leaping moment she thought he had Joe . . . or had some news of him. 'Have you seen . . . do you know . . .' she stared towards him. He looked grave, as he shook his head.

'No, I've only just heard the message, I was standing over there,' he pointed to the show-jumping ring. 'I thought you could use some help. How long has Joe been gone?' he asked.

'Just on fifteen minutes.'

'And where were you when you missed him?'

'At the covered market.' Kit explained what had happened, her mind cleared and she felt more calm. Charles had come to help, they would find Joe; they would join forces and find him.

'He's a sensible boy, and we'll find him,' his voice was normal and strong. 'I'm sure we'll find him, you and I—we'll have a quick scout round now. Have you been to the Highland cattle enclosure? Joe mentioned that, didn't he . . . said you were meeting MacBride there?' He saw Kit's face come alight.

'I haven't tried there,' she all but shouted, 'he'll be there for sure! Oh, why ever didn't I think of that? That's where he'll have gone. He can't tell the time, so he wouldn't have known it was nowhere near five o'clock. There's where he'll be!' They set off over the grass.

Charles's hand moved down and clasped Kit's. 'We'd better keep joined up. There's no sense in you and I losing one another . . . it's easy enough in this crowd.'

She agreed, but castigated herself for not keeping tight hold of Joe. If only I'd kept hold of him while I stood at that stall, she thought. Please let him be at the cattle enclosure, please let him be there, waiting for Hugh . . . don't let him go away!

They reached the enclosure, but didn't see him; they enquired at the various pens. No one had seen a little boy walking around on his own. 'We heard the message from the crêche, of course,' one of the farmers said. 'So he's your boy, is he? Well, if he was mine I'd tell the police right sharp. With crowds like these you never know who might be hanging about.'

Charles's hand tightened round Kit's. 'We'll go back to that stall you were at, but if we haven't found him, say in ten minutes, I think it might be as well to take a trip down to the police station in the centre of the town.' He was trying to say this as calmly and undramatically as he could. 'In the meantime the policewoman on the van here is bound to be on the look-out. He's not been missing *all* that long.'

'Half an hour,' said Kit, just as the crêche official's voice came crackling over the mike again. 'This is a call from the lost children's crêche . . . from the lost children's crêche. Will anyone finding a little boy of five . . .' Kit tried to close her ears. 'Peg and Bob are away, I'm in charge of Joe,' she stared up at Charles. 'How on earth am I going to tell them? I mean, if he's not found soon, how on earth am I going to tell them that he's lost!'

'We'll find him . . . we're going to find him.' He pulled her close to his side. 'We'll go to that stall, and we'll comb the market, most likely he's wandered back there.' But if we have to inform the police, he thought, the Carltons will need to be told, and double-quick. Oh, to hell with all straying, adventurous kids! His expression was grim as once more they pushed through the crowd.

To Kit, whose fear was notching up with every breath she drew, the faces of the jostling crowd had changed from merely indifferent to crafty and sly. Why, even the band had an undercurrent of menace—thump-thump, thump-thump—or was that the beat of her heart? After ten more minutes of fruitless searching and abortive enquires, she and Charles left the funfair and market, and crossed the ground again. 'I think we ought to make that trip to the police station now.' Once again Charles was doing his best to sound unworried and cool. He all but said it was just routine, but stopped himself in time.

They were standing on the perimeter of the ground, near the entrance and exit turnstiles. They were standing apart—the slightest touch would have shattered Kit's composure, which was paper-thin and had panic showing through. 'Yes, all right, we'll go,' she whispered. Then two things happened.

The official began to broadcast his message once again, and a tall woman in a huge straw hat with cherries round the brim came through the gates and approached the turnstiles; she halted to buy a ticket. She was thronged around with latecomers who were still pouring into the grounds, so at first Kit, who had noticed the hat with half her conscious mind, failed to see that the woman had a small boy at her side. They passed through the turnstile, and the boy emerged, walking importantly forward. He was wearing red shorts and a white T-shirt, and he carried a garden gnome. There was a second while Kit stood rooted, stood unbelieving and mute . . . and then she was shouting and running forward. 'Charles, it's him, it's Joe! It's Joe . . . it's him!' She reached him and scooped him up in her arms. 'Joe, oh, *Joe*!' She hugged him tightly, he all but dropped his gnome, he protested loudly and she set him down. 'Wherever have you been? Where have you been . . . oh, how *could* you run off like that?'

'I found him in my garden.' The wearer of the hat regarded Kit from under its brim. 'He'd most likely been there some time. I nap in the afternoons these days, and I woke up and saw him. I live over there in Gnome Cottage.' She swung back a silk-clad arm and pointed out the ornate little house on the other side of the road. 'I'm surprised he didn't get knocked down with all this traffic about.' Her voice held blame, so did her eyes, which also censured Charles.

'Small children occasionally give one the slip,' he

looked lofty and stuck out his chin. He could cheerfully have upended Joe and given his bottom a smack. He considered him spoiled, and Joe—not impervious to vibes—stood close to Kit, who was thanking the woman for bringing him safely back.

'I'd hardly keep him . . . I don't like boys! . . . but on the other hand I couldn't let him cross this appalling road again on his own. He can keep the gnome, I've enough already. Good day to you both.' She turned round to ask the ticket official to refund her entrance money. 'You can't possibly charge me for less than five minutes! Why, I've scarcely set foot on the grass!' She got her refund. Kit and Charles watched her depart.

'You've caused your aunt a great deal of worry,' Charles chided Joe, as they hurried along to the children's crêche before the zealous official could send out his bulletin yet again.

'I wanted to see the Gnome House, and I know how to cross roads.' Joe spoke in jerks, he wanted to go to the loo.

Kit said nothing, for she knew, once she started, she might go on and on. Relief was spiked and spiced with anger. She was furious with her nephew. I could shake him, she thought, but she knew this to be pure gut reaction, so she held her tongue. She would lecture him later on.

'Good, now I can change the record!' the official smiled when he saw them. His wife took one look at Kit and insisted on tea again. Taking her husband, her own children, and Joe outside, she left Charles and Kit to sit down in peace. 'You look fit to drop,' she said.

At first Kit was unwilling to let Joe out of her sight, but in the end sense and reason prevailed; she was tired out of her mind, and the chance to sit down quietly out of the hurly-burly outside was tempting, and anyway, Charles brought pressure to bear. I'm no match for him, she thought. I wonder if he gets his dominance from his father? And what *about* his father, doesn't he want to go and join him? Apparently he didn't; he was pouring the tea and frowning down at the pot. A brimming mug was put in her hands, which he must have noticed were shaking. 'It's a little too soon for you to be having a fright like this,' he said.

'It's not the kind of fright I'd relish at any time!' She smiled and sipped the tea; it was hot and strong and very sweet—the basic treatment for shock! 'It was good of you to join forces with me.'

'I don't think I did very much.'

They were sitting side by side, the tea-tray at their feet, and as the floor of the hut wasn't level the chairs had a slight list. Kit found she was inclining towards Charles, whether she wanted to or not. 'Having someone with me meant a great deal,' she said, and for a few minutes they sat and drank their tea, relaxing in their small oasis of silence ringed around by the noises of the Show.

Kit was beginning to realise the extent of her relief. Joe was safe . . . yes, safe, playing outside at the back of the hut. 'It was so strange,' she said. 'When I spotted him . . . I mean, just now, with that woman. I looked at him, and I knew it was him, yet I couldn't take in what I saw for several seconds; it was just as though my brain wouldn't register properly. It was the same when he disappeared, when he slipped away from that stall. I just stared at the empty space in front of me, I couldn't believe he'd gone. It was like a kind of stupefaction.'

Charles smiled. 'It's called shock,' he told her.

'I wasn't taking proper care of him, was I? That's what's so terrible'—her agitation was coming back—'I should have kept hold of his hand. It was perfectly true what that woman said, anything could have happened!'

'You're blaming yourself.' His words were a statement and he brought them out flatly, with very little expression on his face.

'Is that so surprising?' His lack of sympathy put her on her mettle.

'No, but self-blame is a painful process. I've been through it myself. I once had a small girl left in my charge, during a wedding reception. My attention was caught elsewhere, and she got away from me, down into the hotel drive, practically under a car.'

A pang shot through Kit. She met his eyes and they held hers steadily. She knew what he was referring to—the occasion of Peter Haines' wedding, that never-to-be-forgotten wedding, when Tim *and* she had shown themselves up in such an appalling light. 'I know when you mean,' she said angrily, 'and I would just like to say . . .'

'Don't . . . it's old ground.' Charles's hand touched hers, then moved away again. 'The point I'm trying to make is that at times one is taken off guard. With children in one's care it shouldn't happen, but regrettably it does. Sometimes it does to the best of us . . . even to me, believe it or not!' He was trying to make her laugh. 'I understand what you're feeling,' he added, 'very well indeed.'

He meant what he said, she could see that; his eyes expressed his concern.

'Thank you for telling me—it helps,' she told him.

'Good, I hoped it might.' He removed her empty mug and put it with his on the tray by their chairs. Kit smiled at him, feeling close to him in a way that astonished her. He had made her feel less guilty about Joe; he had also, with consummate tact, let her know that he blamed himself and not her or Tim for what happened at that wedding all of three years ago. It was old ground, and best forgotten, she thought, and felt relief seep into her mind like healing balm.

Charles, moving round on the chair at her side, wondered at her expression. 'Did it really worry you so much, that business at the wedding?' He moved her hair across her face, then tucked it behind her ear. She was mesmerised, held in thrall, she couldn't stop looking at him.

'It worried me, yes, for some time afterwards, and on and off since then.'

'That wedding changed my life,' he said. 'Everything ended there, and began there too. You're so lovely, Kit, do you know that? So beautiful.'

He was going to kiss her, she knew he was, his fingers were under her chin, moving her face to his, and the light in the bungalow-hut was blotted out as he brought his mouth to hers. There was strangeness at first, a first-time feeling . . . the very first time with him, then nothing but pleasure, sharp and strong, sweet and overwhelming, climbing and climbing, up and up. I love him, I love him, I love him, sang in her mind, while her mouth answered his with everything that was in her. Perhaps they would never have heard the sound of footsteps outside, but they both felt the movement the hut gave when their two friends mounted the ramp. There was just time to move apart as Joe flung himself in.

'Aunt Kit, it's time, it's time to go! Dr Mac will be waiting for us! He'll be waiting now, he'll be waiting now . . . it's nearly five o'clock!'

'It's five minutes past,' intoned Charles, picking up the tray.

'Then we'd better go, and fast, hadn't we?' Kit took Joe by the hand. She thanked the official and his wife, but didn't look at Charles; she couldn't not at once. Joe picked his gnome up off the floor, by which time Charles was outside. Kit could see his long shadow thrusting over the grass. There was someone with him . . . why, his father! She had forgotten Mr Niall. She would have to stop and speak to him; she could hardly just whisk by.

The likeness between father and son was strong, she had thought that in the tea tent, but now, outside in the sunshine, it seemed to leap out at her. This is how

Charles will look in thirty years' time, she thought, listening to Mr Niall senior saying how sorry he was that she had had such an alarming afternoon.

'Yes, it was dreadful, but it helped having company. Charles was . . . very supportive,' she told him.

'I'm glad to hear it.' Max Niall had a good look at Kit. It was unlike his son to go chasing round in search of a lost child. On the other hand, perhaps it wasn't. Heaven help us all if he falls into that trap again, he thought. He watched the two of them as they said goodbye, as Kit walked away with Joe.

Kit still felt she had been through a storm, as she crossed the crowded showground. What had happened between Charles and herself must have been a sort of reaction. It was a relief thing, after finding Joe, that was all it had been. And yet she knew it wasn't, she knew it had been much more. There had been hunger in his kiss, and in hers for him; they had wanted one another with desperate urgency, just at that moment; it had been nothing to do with Joe. Still, she needn't worry. Feelings like that were very quickly gone, so she didn't really know how it was that the press of Charles's mouth on hers stayed with her for the rest of the afternoon.

She apologised to Hugh for being late, when they joined him at the enclosure. 'Perhaps it was unavoidable,' he said, looking rather annoyed. He carried Joe's gnome for him, but made no comment on it. He plainly assumed that Kit had bought it for him at the Show. As she didn't want to go over all the business of Joe's disappearance, not quite so soon, she let the matter ride.

They spent another hour at the Show, by which time Joe was tired. Kit's head ached, so did her feet, and she was only too thankful to tumble into Hugh's car and be driven home. Joe fell asleep on the rear seat, curled up with his gnome. When they got to Hilldown, Harriet gave him supper and put him straight to bed. 'Dee's already there,' she told Kit. 'I didn't suppose you would want to be bothered with her, not with the doctor here.' He stayed to supper, she had known he would do so, and the meal she set before them was delicious; she took her place with them, of course.

During the meal Kit told them about Joe's trip to Gnome Cottage. She didn't attempt to play it down, but told them about it in detail, mentioning her fright and Charles Niall's helpfulness. If her voice dropped in cadence and a flush stained her cheeks when she told them of Charles's part in it all, neither of her listeners appeared to notice; they were staring at her aghast.

'Great Scott, Katherine! It could have been serious . . . you should never have let go of his hand!' Hugh laid down his spoon; they were drinking Vichyssoise.

'I'm sure Kit knows that, Doctor.' Harriet passed him the salt, adding that Joe was as slippery as an eel, and apt to take advantage and play up when his parents weren't around.

'I should have kept hold of him, I realise that.' Kit was looking at Hugh. She felt he was about to say something else, but Harriet forestalled him.

'Bob will need to have a talk with the boy, father to son,' she said. 'You'll have to confess to Peg and Bob, dear . . . you can't get out of it.'

'I have every intention of telling them.' Neither Hugh nor Harriet were saying quite what Kit had hoped; she set her chin and said: 'I'd feel underhand if I didn't tell them, and quite apart from that, Joe, at some time or other, would be bound to let it out.'

'Children being what they are, he most certainly would.' Hugh dabbed at his moustache. 'It was good of Niall to come to the rescue. Did you run into him by chance?'

Kit looked at him, then down at her plate. 'Yes, by chance at first,' she said, 'in the tea tent, as a matter of fact. He'd got his father with him. Then when Joe went missing he heard the message given out over the tannoy and he joined me at the crêche.'

'What a good thing you had someone with you.' Harriet brought in the mousse—a shrimp one, with a mixed salad, perfect fare for a summer evening. But out of the three of them she was the only one who really did it justice. Kit and Hugh ate very little, and their conversation was stilted. Perhaps they weren't going together, or anything like that. Harriet thought. She wasn't a selfish woman, no one could call her that, but the last thing she wanted was for her daughter-in-law to remarry. If she did she might not be able to see so much of her darling granddaughter . . . Tim's daughter, and the image of him too.

Kit had said she would never marry again, but she might change her mind. Men abounded in hospitals, and who was this Charles Niall? She would ask Kit about him later on.

CHAPTER EIGHT

KIT was plunged in at the deep end when she went back on duty three weeks later, towards the end of July. It was a Monday and, therefore, one of the main operating days. There were fifteen patients due for surgery, two theatres were in use; a Mrs May Kelland was the first, very serious, patient on Charles Niall's list. From the nursing report, and also from a quick reading of her notes, Kit learned she was suffering from dysphagia —difficulty in swallowing. She was emaciated and very low-spirited. 'I don't care if I do die, Nurse,' she said, as Kit and Jean Holden came into the side-ward to give her her pre-med jab.

'Now that's not fighting talk, Mrs Kelland. Why, in three or four days' time you'll wonder why you said that!' Kit gave her the injection, checked her identity band and covered her up.

On her way back to the clinical room her mind remained on May Kelland. She knew it was very possible that the woman wouldn't pull through. Her husband had been put in the picture, Kit hadn't met him yet, but she couldn't help thinking how terrible he must be feeling right at this moment. Charles Niall was a skilful surgeon, but he couldn't perform miracles, or could he? Dick Parker said he was as good as the Professor, especially as regards oesophageal and upper abdominal surgery. But even if May Kelland survived surgery, the post-operative stage would be tricky, bearing in mind the weak state she was in. She had not consulted her doctor nearly early enough. Surely her husband ought to have made her seek help long before this. Still, I suppose I'm a fine one to criticise, Kit sighed as she remembered her own reluctance to seek professional help.

In the main ward Sister Clive and Dick Parker were completing a short round. Dick would soon be needed in theatre, and was anxious to be gone. Nurse Geare was finishing a blanket-bath and was tucking her patient up; Nurse Barnes, the agency nurse, was giving out mail.

Kit had six more patients to prepare for surgery. Mrs Lena Penn, to whom she went next, was on the Professor's list. She had a large incisional hernia at the site of an old operation. The Professor intended to remove the sac and repair the weakened area with strips of fascia taken from Mrs Penn's thigh. Her leg needed to be shaved from the groin down to below the knee; she made pithy comments while Kit got on with the task. She was a cheerful woman with a blaze of hair permed to a wire wool frizz. The Professor had told her what was to happen, and she had listened to him askance. 'Is the NHS so short of funds, Nurse, that they've run out of thread?' she asked. 'Fancy darning me up with my own skin! Did you ever hear the like?'

'It's called Gallie's operation, and it's often done.' Kit mopped and dried her leg. 'Your thigh will heal in no time at all and your tummy will be strong. You'll have no more trouble; it'll be worth it in the end.'

'Well, I must admit I'm sick of the thing, not to mention my husband. It gets in his way, if you see what I mean . . . spoils his fun and games!' She winked at Kit and gave one last look at the large unsightly protrusion before it was swabbed over and covered with gauze. 'I'm lucky to be in here at all, dear,' she added, as Kit helped her into a gown and fixed a cap over her bush of hair.

The porters arrived to collect Mrs Kelland. Kit accompanied her down to theatres and through into the anaesthetic room. Charles Niall was in there, talking to the anaesthetist. He was in theatre greens, his cap pulled down to rest above his eyebrows; he was masked and his gloved hands were held upwards and away from his body. 'Aren't you rather late?' he enquired of Kit, and then, as though relenting, asked how she was, and backed to the theatre doors, which opened inwards, swallowing him up before she had time to reply.

So much for worrying about meeting him again! she thought, as she left Mrs Kelland with the anaesthetic nurse. She walked up the single flight of stairs leading to Bellingham Ward. She had half dreaded, half looked forward to meeting him again. It was three weeks since that business with Joe, since Charles had supported her through it, and kissed her at the end of it, and Kit had lived and relived that kiss. During the past three weeks, in her less sane moments, she had wondered if he might telephone to ask how she was. But no, he had not, and why should he? Charles had done his part; he had done it well, and retreated abruptly, retreated at speed . . . rather like now, when he had backed through those theatre doors.

'You'll be coming to the Centenary Ball, won't you, Staff?' asked Sheila Barnes, three hours later, up in the staff canteen. 'I've been told I can come, even though I'm not on the permanent staff, and bring a partner. It should be fun, I'm looking forward to it.'

'Yes, I'm coming and, like you, I'm looking forward to it,' Kit said doggedly, breaking a piece of roll.

'Are you asking your consultant friend?'

'Yes, I am, as a matter of fact.'

'He's so good-looking! I adore his beard. He reminds me of a Viking.' Sheila sighed; her boyfriend was an optician in the town. He wasn't good-looking, but his spectacles—he had six different pairs—lent a certain significance to his otherwise nondescript face. Sheila was pressing for marriage in the fairly near future. She was thirty and wanted to settle down.

The Centenary Year Ball would be a very grand affair. Kit had known about it ever since she came to the

General. During her sick leave time at home she had made herself a dress—a creation, Peg called it, for that was what it was. It was a crisp yellow cotton dress, splashed with cornflowers and poppies; the bodice was fitting and strapless, the skirt was full and long. It was a perfect dress for a summer ball . . . 'And no one would ever know that it wasn't a model,' Peg had declared, as she circled round her cousin. It was she who had done all the pinning and painstaking fitting. Peg was a love, she was ever helpful; she was also generous-minded. She had hidden her horror, and not gone on about Kit losing Joe at the Show. Joe had been talked to seriously, and his gnome had been confiscated for a whole month; he was having it back next week.

As to the Ball, it was perfectly true Kit had mentioned it to Hugh, but he would probably have gone in any case, for the staffs of three hospitals within the group had been sent invitation cards. Since her illness, when he had been so kind, she had been out with him several times, but as friends only. She had made that clear. Hugh laughed and accepted her terms. 'We would hardly go out if we weren't friends, surely!' he said, but Hugh was no fool, even if he made Kit feel one, for she *had* felt embarrassed laying down guidelines with someone like him. She was never entirely able to forget she had once worked for him at his house.

Charles would be at the Ball, she supposed, and with him would come Faith, with her beautiful bones and gorgeous hair, looking like a princess. Perhaps he would marry her one day, and Faith would still run her shops, and regale him with amusing stories about eccentric customers, taking his mind off the grimmer side of his job.

May Kelland was back in the side-ward when Kit returned from lunch. Nurse Holden had been told to sit with her, and she was looking a little scared; her relief was plain to see when Kit appeared. Mrs Kelland was on underwater seal drainage to ensure proper lung expansion. The free end of the long drain was immersed in a bottle of water—sterile water—which was placed on the floor by her bed. As Jean Holden hadn't seen a water-seal drain in position before, Kit explained how the tube led from the pleural cavity into the bottle, well down below the water level, to act as a value, thereby making a seal. When Mrs Kelland inhaled, the water rose in the tube, when she breathed out it fell again, and this inter-tube oscillation gave an indication of the movement within her chest. 'But it's vital not to kink the tube, and if you move the bottle, never lift it higher than the bed, or you'll run into trouble—water could easily siphon back into her chest.'

'I shan't touch it . . . *ever*!' Jean looked horrified.

'You may have to when we're lifting her for bed-making and toileting. Remember, she came up in the lift with it, there would have been enough movement then. If the bottle has to be emptied or changed, then the tubing must be clamped.'

'Could you come into the office, Staff?' asked Sister from the doorway. 'You stay with the patient, Nurse Holden; she'll be rousing again very soon.'

In the office was Charles, still in his theatre clothes, sitting down and looking uncomfortably warm. And it must, thought Kit, be stifling in all that wrapping. He had four more patients on his list before he was finished, one of them a difficult kidney case. 'I came up with Mrs Kelland,' he said, looking directly at Kit. 'I'm glad to say it was possible to remove the obstruction complete. If she gets thorough the next few days, she'll live her life span and more, but she's going to need expert care and supervision by someone well used to chest and abdominal nursing procedures.'

'Mr Niall would like you to special her, Staff,' Sister broke in at that point. 'When you're off duty I'll take over, so your hours won't be changed.' She added this quickly before Kit could say, on a wave of elation, that she would work all hours, if necessary, till the patient was over the worst. Staff Nurse Tennant was only just back from sick leave herself. Sister believed in a sense of duty, but not an excess of it. If she read the signs aright the fact that May Kelland was Charles Niall's patient had something to do with her staff nurse's willingness to work herself into the ground. Sister's cutting off tactics worked, as they nearly always did. Kit merely said she would be very glad to special Mrs Kelland, and went out feeling as though she was walking on air. As she explained to Peg when she got home that evening, to be asked to special a patient *was* special, you couldn't help feeling proud.

'So it's an accolade, is it?' Peg leaned back on the swing garden seat. The evening was warm; she was waiting for Bob to come home.

'In a way it is.' Kit got up with Dee, it was time for her bath and bed. 'You feel you're trusted professionally, and it's better for the patient to have one nurse looking after her . . . that is if she takes to you. Not that I think Mrs Kelland has taken to any of us much. I hope she's not going to be one of those people who don't *try* to get well. Quite apart from her illness I don't think she's a very happy person.'

'Whereas you're over the moon to be asked by that stunning Charles Niall to be asked to special one of his patients.' Peg's look was a little arch.

'I'm pleased to be asked, I don't know about jumping over the moon,' replied Kit. 'I like to feel that he thinks I'm up to the job, that's all.'

'Don't fall in love with him,' Peg called after her cousin's retreating back. Kit turned round, holding Dee.

'What's that supposed to mean?'

'Exactly what I say, Kit . . . don't fall in love with Charles Niall. I don't think he's the kind of man to want to get seriously involved with any woman, not in the long term. Faith Melville can handle him, or she looks as though she can, but I think he's one of those toughie types who gets most of his satisfactions from achievement . . . and I'm talking of his work.'

'You seem to have got him neatly docketed, and I'm not a complete fool, Peg.' Not trusting herself to say any more, Kit resumed her journey into the house. There were times when Peg saw too much.

Walter Kelland came to visit his wife the following afternoon. Kit asked him not to stay too long, nor to talk to her very much. 'I know that's a funny thing to say, Mr Kelland, but she is still very ill.'

'I was told that her operation was entirely successful.' He came close to Kit when he spoke; he was very sure of himself; good-looking in a saturnine way, with black, close-set eyes that stared into hers, then looked her up and down. 'So don't tell me,' he continued, 'that it's going to be one of those cases in which the surgery was brilliant, but the hapless patient died.'

'Of course not!' Kit backed away; they were in the corridor. She was shocked, not only by his words, but by the way he delivered them, smiling unpleasantly, still looking her up and down. Quickly she opened the side-ward door. 'Here's your husband, Mrs Kelland.' She pulled out a chair and left him there, but she also left the door open and busied herself in the office opposite. I'll give him ten minutes, then go back in and ask him to leave, she thought. What's the use of being a special nurse if I don't assert myself? As it happened she didn't have to, for he left after only five minutes, looking impatient, looking at his watch, shouldering his way through the tide of visitors coming in from the lifts.

It was after the proper visiting time when he came next day. The physiotherapist was with Mrs Kelland, encouraging her to continue to practise her breathing exercises. Kit went along to the waiting-room to explain this to Walter Kelland. She found him gazing out of the window, hands behind his back, looking dark and dapper in a navy blazer and pale grey slacks. Yet there was something unpleasant about him, and Kit felt a creeping sensation prickle her skin as he turned at her approach. 'I'm too late to see my wife, am I? Is that what you've come to say?' As he spoke he began to walk towards her, while his close-set eyes, like black beetles, travelled all over her.

The insolence of his stare annoyed her, but she did her level best not to show it in her face as she told him that the physiotherapist was with his wife, which meant he would have to wait. 'It should only be a matter of minutes,' she added, 'but you *are* a little late.'

'I was busy,' he smiled at her; she smelled whisky on his breath, 'but I'm sure I shan't mind waiting in such charming company as yours.'

'I have patients to attend to.' She turned away.

'I thought you were specialling my wife.' As he spoke he brushed past her and blocked the way between her and the passage outside. The door was half open and he leaned against it, clicking it quietly shut. 'Pay forfeit, and I'll let you go!' He folded his arms and laughed, still leaning backwards on the door; he was more drunk than she had thought.

'Mr Kelland, please let me pass!' Kit stepped forward and he grabbed her, gripped her upper arms and held her fast. Instinct told her not to struggle, to struggle would fire his mood. His smile had gone and his eyes were hot, his fingers were iron bands. And yet . . . and yet he didn't draw closer. There was space between them still and it didn't lessen, so perhaps even he, in his alcoholic haze, lacked the final courage to use more force. 'Take your hands off me at once, Mr Kelland, and stand away from the door!' Her voice was clear, not exactly loud, but pitched quite high enough to make him realise that if he persisted she would raise it to a shout and bring in whoever was passing by.

'You can't take a joke, can you, you silly little fool!' His look was venomous, but he let her go, and moved away from the door. Kit opened it, passed into the corridor and up to the linen room, where she sat amidst the walls of sheets, rubbing her upper arms and trying to control the shaking of her limbs. It was childish to be so upset. She told herself to buck up . . . you're all right, it's all over, you handled him all right. He'd had too much to drink, and he's beastly anyway, but there's no harm done.

And in all these respects but one, she was right—in all but the last one—for Walter Kelland was the type of man who always got his own back; his vindictive streak was the strongest one he had.

The physiotherapist waylaid Kit in the corridor, as she was making her way back. 'Your patient is free now, Staff,' she said, 'but she doesn't want to see her husband. She says she's too tired. Sister's in the waiting-room explaining all this to him. It's fairly unusual for husbands and wives not to want to see one another. There's no trouble between them, is there?' Her lugubrious face didn't quite hide her curiosity.

'I've no idea.' Kit glanced back just in time to see Sister Clive and Walter Kelland come out of the waiting-room and push through the doors to the lifts. Sister had no doubt been tact itself; she wouldn't have got herself into the silly situation that Kit had done. But now someone else was coming in, and despite all her resolutions not to be affected by him, Kit felt her spirits soar at the sight of Charles Niall striding towards her, white coat loose as usual, a bundle of folders under his arm.

'Good afternoon, ladies,' he greeted them both, but it was Kit he was looking at. The physiotherapist would have liked a few words with him, but he swept into the side-ward, calling out, 'Ready when you are, Staff,' plainly in a hurry.

But there was no evidence of hurry when he

approached Mrs Kelland's bed, and he took the trouble to sit down too, which meant she could talk to him at eye level, without having to crane her neck. He sat at the side of the bed where the water-seal bottle was placed. He was able to watch the rise and fall of water in the tube. There was good movement, so no impairment of diaphragm function, and no bubbling, either, which meant no air in the pleural space. Even so he wasn't entirely happy about her condition. Most patients, unless too ill to bother, asked questions about themselves. May Kelland didn't. Charles pointed down at the bottle on the floor. 'We'll have you off that at the weekend, and off your gastric tube too. By then you'll be taking food by mouth and have no trouble getting it down. You understand, don't you,' he leaned towards her, 'that you *are* completely cured. You won't have any recurrence of your trouble . . . that's all in the past.'

Mrs Kelland nodded and said that she did understand, but she made no other comment. Charles watched her closely. She was apathetic, practically couldn't-care-less. From a patient so weakened by illness he had not expected a whoop of delight; what he had hoped to see was some lessening of anxiety in her thin face, some show of relief in her eyes.

'She's depressed,' he said worriedly to Kit in the office. 'It could be her drugs, I suppose.' He frowned and looked at her treatment sheet, running his thumb down the numerous items on the list. 'I don't want to take her off anything, nor reduce the dosage yet. She hasn't complained of pain, has she?' he lifted his eyes to Kit.

'She hasn't complained of anything, except dryness of mouth.'

'That will solve itself once she starts oral feeding. In the meantime I'll write her up for an antibiotic mouthwash, which will help to a certain extent.' Charles reached out for the prescription pad, while Kit stood at the side of the desk, staring at his downbent head as he took the top off his pen. It was so good to be working with him like this, so good to feel that he trusted her, absolutely, with the care of his patient; the mere fact of his presence made the scene with Walter Kelland fade away in her mind. 'Are you coming to the Centenary bash tonight?' he asked as he signed the single prescription and stood up ready to go.

'Yes, I am. Are you?' Kit moved back to allow him to get to the door, but he seemed in no great hurry for once; he perched on the edge of the desk.

'I am, because in a way it will be useful for me,' he said. 'I'll be able to meet colleagues from other hospitals in the group. I didn't come here till February, you know, so I'm a fairly new lad. There are still a number of folk I don't know—telephoning and writing aren't quite the same as meeting them in the flesh.'

'I know exactly what you mean,' smiled Kit, 'and the same applies to me—to a lesser extent,' she added quickly, not wanting him to think she was putting herself on a par with him . . . heaven forbid!

'I know MacBride is coming, I saw him in Boots yesterday.'

'Oh yes, he is, but then quite a crowd are coming from St Margaret's. I'm looking forward to meeting them again. I nursed there for six months. That was before I had Dee.'

'I remember you telling me that,' said Charles, just as Sister came into the room.

'Mr Kelland seemed more relieved than sorry not to see his wife. One wonders what kind of marriage they've got.' Sister edged behind her desk and sat down; her feet were killing her.

'Some people are alarmed by the sight of illness.' Charles moved to the door. 'Once May Kelland is off all tubes, and looks less scary, her husband will be first in the queue, as keen as all the rest!'

'For a medical man, Mr Niall, you have great faith in human nature,' said Sister with such acerbity that Kit fell to wondering if she viewed Walter Kelland in much the same way as herself.

Sister Clive was the first person Kit and Hugh spoke to when they entered the ballroom of the Queen's Hotel, just after eight-thirty that night. Kit couldn't get over how appealing she looked in her pale blue dress. It was velvet, so perhaps rather heavy for a dance on a warmish night, but it was cleverly cut and showed off her figure, which was curvy in all the right places. Her hair was pretty, a rich dark brown, set in curls all over her head. It was amazing how very different people looked out of uniform. They were apt to behave differently too, and Sister was no exception. She was bubbly and buoyant, and looked less than her thirty-two years. She was with the Professor, who matched her in mood. 'My wife hasn't come,' he explained, 'she doesn't like hospital functions. No sense in forcing her . . . couldn't do that, it's not my way.' He asked Kit to dance . . . pop music, he told her, was very much his style. 'My son has all the latest albums, I like to keep up to date.'

Hugh was dancing with Sister, Kit could see them as they turned. They were dancing well, even expertly, but were not attempting to twist and sway and let-it-all-go-slack, like most of the other dancers—like, for instance, the Professor, who was flinging Kit about as though he were twenty and Superman, not sixty-three and a surgeon—a puffing surgeon. Kit feared for him, and was greatly relieved when the Dazzlers pop group, in sequinned suits, changed to a smoochy number, when slow-and-dreamy took over from jig-and-fling.

Halfway through this number Charles and Faith came in. They began to dance immediately, and were lost amongst the crowd; then suddenly they were in view again, a short way from Kit and the Prof. They waved, so did Kit, and the Professor beamed. 'Good-looking woman, that!' He meant Faith, of course. Kit agreed with him.

Faith was more dramatic-looking than ever, with her gold hair hanging loose. Her dress was aquamarine and shiny, slim and long in the skirt, tapering to a kind of tail of knife pleats at the back. She looked like a beautiful mermaid clinging to her rock—the rock being Charles, they were dancing close, and Kit averted her eyes. The Professor, however, manoeuvred near them, so that when the music stopped they were all four standing together. Faith commented on Kit's dress.

'I'm quite sure you didn't buy *that* in Bewlis!'

'That's true, I didn't,' smiled Kit, giving nothing away, but feeling distinctly thrown when Faith pirouetted in her fishtail dress, and said she had made it herself.

'Without a pattern, and with no one to fit me. I pulled it out of the sky, or out of the sea!' Once more she fanned out the tail.

'Most ingenious . . . a superb effort!' The Professor praised her lavishly. Charles agreed that Faith was clever, and the Professor asked her to dance.

'Faith is very artistic, isn't she?' remarked Kit in over-bright tones.

'She is, but without the mercurial temperament that sometimes goes with it.' Charles took her hand. 'Let's dance, shall we? MacBride is still deep in talk with Sister Clive, and a thin chap in glasses, whom I seem to have met before.'

'That will be Sheila Barnes' boyfriend.' Kit slid into his arms.

'And Sheila's taking the floor with Dick.' For some reason Charles seemed to think that a commentary on who was with whom, and why, was of interest to Kit. The truth was she couldn't have cared less if the room had been packed with chimps. She was only concerned with the fact that she was with him. He held her closely as they moved off to the throbbing beat of the drums. Her chin came to where his tucked evening shirt met the black of his bow tie; her forehead levelled with his mouth, she could see the side of his cheek, the way his jaw moved when he spoke, she could feel his hand at her waist. 'You look very, very decorative in your summer meadow dress,' he said softly, close against her ear.

'I'm glad you approve.'

'I do . . . I do!' He drew her closer still.

'I made it myself, so in that respect Faith and I are level pegging!' she said lightly leaning back to smile into his face.

'Don't toy with me, Kit, I can't stand it!' he said, and his tone wasn't light at all. He looked strained and intense, and the lines on his face stood out like pencil marks. He missed a step; she all but fell, and he tightened his grip round her waist. 'I'm sorry, that was my fault—I'm not in good form tonight, unlike MacBride who dances as though he's been doing it all his life.'

'He's enjoying himself, don't knock him for that!'

'Sorry again,' he said. Shock at her swift comeback sat in his eyes for a second, followed by another expression that was just as quickly gone, and replaced by the bland one that always frustrated her. 'After I've met whom I need to meet, Faith and I will call it a day or, more aptly, a night, I suppose.' His glance went to the windows already framing the first purplish shadows of dusk. 'Dancing half the night, through,' he added, 'isn't my idea of fun after a day spent mostly on my feet.'

'The Professor wouldn't agree with you, he's intent on staying the course.' And now Kit felt stiff and ill at ease—more than that, she felt wretched. Was it her, or Charles, or some devilish imp dancing in between them, making all this tension, winding them on the wrong thread?

'The Professor and I don't agree on all issues,' Charles

said quietly. There was a slackening of his defences then, a change in his attitude; she sensed him turning towards her, and felt he might have gone on and said more, but somehow or other the moment eluded their grasp . . . perhaps because the music stopped, and other people joined them. Dick Parker asked Kit for the next dance, and Charles went to talk to Sheila and her bony boy-friend, who was stronger than he looked.

'You're slipping tonight,' Dick grinned at Kit.

'What do you mean by that?'

'You're sliding down the status scale.' Dick danced like an acrobat. Seemingly never short of breath, he explained what he meant. 'First you go to the top of the tree and pluck off our merrie consultant, on the next bough you snaffle his registrar, and now, alas and alack, you have to make do with the houseman on the humblest branch of all.'

'Well, I have to mix with the common herd most of the time, you know!' Kit laughed, her bell of bright hair swinging from side to side, as she followed Dick's movements. She tried not to think of Charles.

'No one would ever guess that we were meant to be together,' grumbled Hugh, a little later on, when he and Kit joined up.

'It's a dance, and I know a lot of people.'

'I couldn't help noticing that.'

'But you've been all right, haven't you?' She knew that he had, she had seldom seen him so relaxed, so taken out of himself. Hugh had been meeting old friends, both from the Bewlis General, and from the Throat and Ear Hospital on the other side of town.

'I'm all right *now*,' he said with emphasis, leading her on to the floor. Hugh felt settled in his mind, for he had come to a decision. He had therefore been released from that backwards and forwards state, when neither course seemed exactly right, and the middle one was stalemate. Coming here this evening had clarified his thoughts.

'You're looking very lovely, Katherine.' His beard brushed Kit's cheek, as he turned to face her; he was slightly less tall than Charles.

'Thank you for the compliment!' she smiled.

'It's meant, I assure you.'

As she caught his look, a thread of anxiety began to tug and ring warning bells in Kit's mind. She closed her ears to them; she was being silly. Hugh was simply enjoying himself. Why, he probably had the same look in his eye when he danced with Sister Clive. It was the music . . . it was titillating; it was also enormous fun. She gave herself up to the pleasure of dancing with him.

At one point, as he turned her, she found herself looking at Charles, whose eyes met hers over the top of Sheila Barnes' nut-brown head. An expression of cynical amusement sat heavily on his face, then vanished as Sheila spoke to him, as he turned his head to her. Faith was with Dr Manders, who was clearly under her spell.

'I suppose,' remarked Kit, as she and Hugh went into the supper-room, 'that you'd call Faith Melville a femme fatale.'

'Some people might. I dare say.'

Charles and Faith were already sitting at one of the damask-clothed tables set for six people. Sister Hart and her husband, Carl Manders and Sister Martin from A and E were with them; Faith appeared to be making them laugh. 'My guess is,' said Hugh, as he and Kit queued at the buffet table, 'that underneath all that glamour and gaiety, Miss Melville is a very shrewd lady, who knows exactly what and whom she wants.'

'You could be right.' Bob had called her shrewd. Kit chose a wedge of quiche with green salad, and waited for Hugh who was having ham off the bone. By the time they worked their way back to the tables most of them were taken, but there were two places left at the Prof's table. He beckoned and called them over. He was with

Sister Clive, and a married couple—both doctors—from St Margaret's, whom Hugh knew. They settled down to talk. The table was no more than two yards from the one Charles and Faith occupied. Charles's back was to Kit, and so was Faith's, for the tables were round. Kit could almost forget they were there at all, for the Professor's broad chest blotted out much of her forward view. Nevertheless, she didn't forget them, not for a single second. During a lull in the talk at her own table, she found herself straining her ears to hear what Charles and company were saying at theirs. They were discussing, she discovered, the boating accident that had occurred at Brighton a few days ago, when three young men had been drowned.

'The trouble is,' Carl Manders was saying, 'far too many people think sailing is a doddle, that any fool can do it, and they couldn't be more wrong. The sea can be a deadly foe, unless treated with respect.'

'I couldn't agree more,' Sister Hart's husband said.

'It's the young wives, the widows, I'm sorry for,' Sister Martin exclaimed. 'One of them is only twenty, only married a month, and the other two have young children.'

'Shocking for them,' said Faith.

'One wonders,' and now Charles was talking, 'how they ever get over it. On the other hand, it's a well-known fact that the female species are tough. Most young widows marry again; they set out to do so, especially if they have a child, or children to support.'

'Who can blame them?' said Sister Martin.

'Who indeed?' agreed Charles. 'I don't blame them, just steer clear of them!' This raised a general laugh. Kit stiffened, then said, 'Hark at him!' to Hugh in an aside, but *in*side she was furious. It was all she could do to stop herself going to the next table and having it out with him. He had known she was sitting not far behind him, well within earshot. Had he said it for fun, as a cheap sort of joke, or was it a subtle warning, levelled at her, not to get ideas about him? He had meant her to hear, she was sure of it, or was she getting paranoid? She was glad when Hugh said he wanted to go back to dance.

Shortly after that they decided to go home. When they got back to Hilldown . . . they walked the short distance . . . Kit suggested that Hugh rang for a taxi to take him on to his house at Cawnford. 'But stay and have a drink, if you like—a cup of coffee, or something.' She didn't sound very pressing, but he appeared not to notice; he opted for coffee and she made him the instant kind. As she brought it into the sitting-room, he rose and took the tray.

'Just to put the record straight, Katherine,' he said, as they sat down, 'I thought Niall's remarks about young widows were pretty fatuous.'

'He's entitled to his opinion,' was all she could manage to say. The anger she had felt when Charles made his views known had faded off; all she felt was chilly and upset. The coffee did nothing to warm her, and she was glad when a cry from the bedroom allowed her to escape Hugh's presence. She lifted Dee from her cot. 'What's the matter, darling? Did we wake you up?' The child's solid weight, the butt of her head, and her chirps of glee, were all that was needed to settle her mother and restore her confidence.

'Is she all right?' Hugh had finished his coffee, but he didn't look ready to go.

'She's fine—she just wanted attention, that's all. I've put her back in her cot.'

'She wanted her mother, and I don't blame her.' He made room for Kit on the settee. 'You're a good mother, I've always thought you've a way with children, you know. But she would be better off with two parents. A child needs a father.'

'That's a fairly obvious statement, Hugh.' Kit wasn't alerted at first to the possible significance of his remark, till he took her hand in his. The truth winged home then. 'If Tim hadn't been killed,' she said quickly, withdrawing her hand, 'Dee would have had her father, but he was killed, wasn't he, and I don't mean to remarry just to give her a second parent, nor even for my own sake, because it doesn't happen to be what I want at all.' She all but gabbled the last few words, for she had to close all doors. Without conceit, but with clear sight, and with startled, awful dismay, she realised that Hugh had been on the brink of proposing to her. She had the sensation of being caught, of a net falling over her head, and she knew that if she didn't think quickly and say something totally blocking, he might persist, and then hate her for turning him down. '*Not* being in love is a kind of freedom, one that I mean to keep.' This time her words came a little more lightly, but the air about their heads was heavy and loaded with things unsaid, while Hugh sat and looked at his knees, then at the rug, then back again at her.

'You sound very feverish about this, Katherine. What are you trying to do . . . disprove Charles Niall's statement?'

'It has nothing to do with him!'

'I wonder.' He got up and crossed the room to the hall. 'I'll walk back into the town, and get a cab from the all-night rank.' He eyed her coldly, reaching for the door.

'You're very welcome to phone from here.' How she wished this hadn't happened!

'Thank you, but there's no need for that. The walk will do me good.' He couldn't wait to be gone, for of course he knew she had read what was in his mind. She knew he had been about to propose, to ask her to share his life. She was right for him . . . young, charming, ladylike and strong. She would have given him children, the family he wanted, she could have shared his considerable comforts, his luxurious home, the prestige attached to his job. He wasn't a mere nobody, and yet she had turned him down. Oh, not in so many words, perhaps, but she had made herself very plain. The realisation of this was bitter. What in heaven's name *did* she want? All that talk of freedom, he didn't believe it for one moment. 'I'll be in touch.' He turned round on the steps.

'Of course,' smiled Kit, and managed to say that she had enjoyed the evening. But Hugh wouldn't get in touch again, she knew that and so did he. It was simply one of those things to say when parting in a hurry, or parting for always. She couldn't help feeling sad.

CHAPTER NINE

NEXT DAY being a Thursday meant that Kit was at home. She did the usual Thursday chores—washing and ironing, gardening and shopping, and taking care of Joe as well as Dee. Peg went on a day trip to Surrey to see her father and mother. In the last-minute rush to get the coach—Peg never allowed enough time—she failed to notice how quiet Kit was, so no searching questions were asked. Kit didn't want to talk about the dance, which she hadn't enjoyed very much, nor mention the break-up with Hugh, which she knew Peg would deplore. A day with the two children for company was exactly what was needed to take her mind off everything but their wants and demands; they drove her mad, but stopped her thinking too much.

She was on late duty on Friday—from twelve-thirty till nine—but she got to the ward a little before midday. She had had to use the bus, as her car was at the garage having its MOT overhaul. As she zipped herself into her uniform dress in the nurses' locker-room, she decided to look in on Mrs Kelland before reporting to Sister. She supposed Walter Kelland would be along, later on. It's a pity I've got to see him, but that's life, she told herself. I dare say I'll weather it. She stepped out into the corridor, and in doing so came face to face with Charles. She spoke, but he didn't answer; he was on his way to the lifts. She felt that although he was looking straight at her, he was on another planet, and if he saw her, didn't register who she was. She spoke again, quite loudly, and he turned and came back to her.

'You've lost your specialling job,' he said, without greeting or preamble.

'Why?' said Kit, equally bluntly, but a shoot of alarm set her heart racing. What had happened? Had May Kelland died?

'Mrs Kelland is in Intensive Care, she had a heart attack yesterday. Sister will fill you in with the details—she was with her when it happened.' He made to pass her, but she stood in his way, scarcely aware that she did so.

'Will she be all right? How is she today?'

Charles's face tightened even more. 'She went into atrial fibrillation. She's in pretty poor shape today. Now, if you'll please let me pass . . .' As she still didn't move, he placed a firm hand on each of her shoulders and slid her away like a door.

'I'm sorry,' she said, 'I wasn't thinking.' But she said it to his back. He had four patients to see in Kilross, and an outpatients' clinic starting at two, which could easily go on for hours.

'It was totally unexpected,' said Sister, when she told Kit about May Kelland. 'All day yesterday, up until teatime, her condition was stable. Dick Parker removed her water-seal drain and her gastric tube. She took a little food by mouth—it went down like a dream. We were all pleased, including her, she really seemed to perk up. Her husband came at visiting-time and was informed of her progress. Then, when I went in to do her obs, just before I went off duty, I noticed her pulse was irregular. I didn't like her colour, so I bleeped Mr Niall, who came quite quickly, but she'd collapsed by the time he got here. She's in ICU, and her condition is only fair.'

'But will she be all right?'

Sister shrugged expressively. 'That's anybody's guess. She's been put on a course of digoxin to slow and strengthen her heartbeat. If digitalisation is produced and maintained, I suppose she may pull through, but if she does, and comes back here . . . I mean into Bellingham Ward, it won't be for ten days or two weeks, which means we've got a bed free. Mr Niall wants to admit a Mrs Valdim for splenectomy. He's seeing her in OPD today, and if she agrees, she will come in at midday tomorrow and be put on Monday's list.' She caught sight of Kit's face, and said quickly and brusquely, 'Don't look like that, Staff. You know only too well what the bed-state is, we can't afford not to take advantage of every situation that leaves one free.'

'But, Sister, supposing . . .'

'*If* May Kelland survives her attack and comes back here before Mrs Valdim is ready for discharge, then room will be made for her if I have to put up an extra bed out in the corridor. Now, does that make you feel any better?' Sounding just faintly sarcastic, Sister went on to deal with the rest of the report. She had had a trying morning, and was anxious to get off duty. She was also, although she would never have admitted it, upset about May Kelland. Her collapse had been a very distressing one.

During the two hours before visiting time, Kit went into the ward. Mrs Penn, the incisional hernia patient, raised a languid arm. On her fourth post-operative day, she was still feeling 'knocked for six'. 'It's taken all the stuffing out of me, dear . . . even my hair don't frizz!' It didn't, it still blazed with colour, but clung to her head like a cap.

'It'll come up for air, like you will, after the weekend,' smiled Kit. On Charles Niall's instructions, Mrs Penn wasn't ambulant yet, merely being encouraged to move her legs and do abdominal exercises, as instructed by the physiotherapy team.

'It's not that I *want* to get out of bed, dear,' Mrs Penn tried to explain, 'but most of the other patients seem to stagger about, and go to the loo, a day or two after their ops.'

'I know, but you had a very large hernia, as well you know, and Mr Niall wants the repair to strengthen before you get on your feet. Everything is going along as expected, and you don't feel *too* bad, do you?'

'Oh no, dear, I mustn't grumble, must I? There's plenty worse off than me . . . like her next door, poor little thing.' Mrs Penn lowered her voice. In the next bed, Shirley Dixon, a young woman of twenty-five, was recovering after the removal of a kidney . . . she had been in a road accident. Her boyfriend was in the orthopaedic unit with leg fractures. He was lucky to be alive. Shirley couldn't understand why the two of them couldn't be together.

'I thought they had male and female patients in the same ward these days.' She looked miserably at Kit, as she went to talk to her.

'They do, in some hospitals,' Kit replied, 'but we're not that advanced here yet. But even if we were, general surgical patients and orthopods wouldn't be mixed. When you're feeling more like it, though, you can write your friend a note. I'd take it down to the ortho floor for you.'

'*Would* you?'

'Of course I would.'

'Thanks, that means a lot.' Shirley's tears ran down the sides of her face.

Kit handed her a tissue from the box on her locker. 'There you are—mop up. Every day makes a difference after an op, you know. You're still in the very early stage, so you're bound to be feeling low.'

'Keith and I were getting married in September. I doubt if we'll manage that now. Still, I suppose we could make it by Christmas.' Shirley composed herself for her rest before the start of visiting, when her mother and brother would come. She had a tiny face framed in chocolate brown hair, her eyes were round and blue, like a Siamese kitten's. Kit wondered what her boyfriend was like. However detached you thought you were about patients in your care, an element of identifying with them, and suffering along with them, *could* creep in, especially if they were in your own age group—it could have been me, was one of the thoughts that occurred.

There was a new patient in bed number twelve, a peptic ulcer case, due to undergo surgery in two days' time. Sister had asked Kit to explain her case to Learner Nurse Holden, and to make sure she witnessed the pre-operative procedures that were being carried out. With this in mind Kit had Jean Holden with her when she took a specimen of Mrs Fyne's blood for grouping and hgb estimation. 'If the labs find her haemoglobin to be low,' she explained in the clinical room,' she'll be transfused before she goes down to theatre. Now, I'm sure you know the type of operation she's having.'

'Yes, Staff . . . a gastrectomy.'

'A *partial* gastrectomy. It's one of the most common abdominal operations. Once she recovers she'll be able to eat normal meals again, perhaps slightly smaller helpings than before, but she won't have any discomfort.'

'Does she know that?'

'Oh yes, Mr Niall has explained everything to her. She's been coming to Outpatients for some weeks now, she's been waiting for a bed. And that reminds me, will you make up the bed in side-ward one. A Mrs Valdim, for splenectomy, is being admitted tomorrow . . . that is if Mr Niall has managed to talk her round to it.'

Mr Niall had, and he brought Ava Valdim's notes up to Bellingham Ward just after eight-thirty that night, which surprised all the nurses. Kit and Jill Geare had just finished the drugs round, evening drinks were being prepared in the ward kitchen, and Kit was checking charts. 'My goodness, you're late!' She gave a start when he plunged into the office.

'It happens,' he said, but when she ventured to ask how May Kelland was, he turned from the door, closed it, came back and sank down in a chair. 'There's not much change, no improvement. Her husband is with her. He's been told he can visit more or less when he likes.'

'She's not a happy woman,' said Kit.

'If by that you mean she's depressed, I think we agreed on that before.' Once more Charles's comment was sharp.

'I don't think she wants to go on living.'

'It's our job to keep her alive.'

'I know that.' Kit swallowed; she mustn't answer him back, at least not too obviously. 'I would like to see her myself. I had thought of going tonight when I sign off duty, but perhaps if Mr Kelland is there I'll leave it for the time being,' she added quietly, putting her charts in a pile.

'I think that would be the better course.' Her clearing-up movements weren't missed by Charles, who went on to tell her about Mrs Ava Valdim. 'She's been living in the Persian Gulf since her marriage fifteen years ago. She's had several bouts of malaria, which have left her with a condition called splenomegaly.' He glanced at Kit, one fair eyebrow raised.

'Enlarged spleen,' she supplied promptly, she knew he was testing her out.

'*Grossly* enlarged, in her case, it's restricting her diaphragm movements. She's on my list for Monday, but as you won't be here for two days the pre-operative tests and procedures will fall to someone else.'

Kit held her tongue with an effort, for perhaps he didn't mean to sound as though she was never there when her help was needed most. She gave him the benefit of the doubt, while knowing full well that no doubt existed . . . he was having a go at her. But perhaps, in a way, it was just as well that he had this maddening streak, for it effectively put distance between them, which maybe he intended, bearing in mind his chauvinist words about widows at the dance. He probably thinks I'm stalking him, she thought. Well, he'll soon find that I'm not. Kit stared at him coldly, watching him get to his feet.

As he opened the door she heard the two night nurses coming down the corridor. 'Enjoy your weekend,' he said over his shoulder, and she assured him that she would. The two nurses came in as he went out.

'He really is *the* most gorgeous chunk of man!' Staff Nurse Rogers rolled her eyes ceilingwards.

'Yes, isn't he?' It was quicker to agree. Kit gave the hand-over report; ten minutes later she was crossing the hospital yard.

It was raining, it would be, of course . . . a thick, fine drizzle that clung to her hair and lashes, and dampened her cardigan, which was all she was wearing over her uniform dress. She could see the bus, like a lit-up galleon, standing at the terminus, and was making tracks for it when a car stopped on its way through the gates. Its headlamps had picked out her hurrying figure, its driver had been surprised to see her on foot. 'What's happened to your car?' Charles opened his passenger door.

'It's being overhauled.' She wanted to keep walking, but manners made her halt. She kept her eye fixed on the bus.

'Get in, I'll drive you,' he said.

She looked at him sitting there, leaning sideways, his hand securing the door. The temptation to do as he said and get in was like a tangible pull. To get in beside him in the warm darkness, to be with him just for a time, to be with him with no one else there, to dream a little and hope a little . . . couldn't do any harm, surely it couldn't. But she knew otherwise, and somehow she stood her ground. 'There's no need to take you out of your way, the bus is there waiting,' she said.

The door opened wider. 'As it happens, I'm going past Mount Cliff Road tonight. Now jump in, you're getting wet, and holding up the traffic.' One or two horns were pipping behind; other hospital personnel had homes to go to, they had all had a long, hard day.

'I must get the bus.' Kit moved back from the car. 'I'm . . . I'm meeting someone on it.' The fib was of the white lie variety, but it got her off the hook.

'In that case, good night.' Charles closed the door and the car moved through the gates, followed by three others. Kit ran across to the bus. It had nearly filled up. She paid her fare and climbed to the top deck. She was so busy wondering if Charles had seen through her ploy to escape him that she didn't notice the other passengers, and was unaware of the fact that Walter Kelland was sitting behind her; he too had got on at the gates. She had been oblivious of her surroundings when she slipped into her seat. He had seen her, though, and recognised her . . . that stuck-up little madam who had slapped him down the other day and looked at him with contempt. No one looked at him like that and got away with it! His anger recharged as he sat and stared at the back of her glossy head, at the curve of her cheek as she turned to the window, at her hand as she cleared the pane. He got off the bus two stops before she did, and by then he had worked out how he could make trouble for her, do a bit of stirring, make her job less cushy for a time . . . special bloody nurse! His face was ugly as he bowed it before the rain.

For Kit it was by no means the happiest of weekends. Peg and she quarrelled, which was something neither could remember doing before. It happened just after lunch on Saturday, when Bob had gone off to his golf. They were sitting in the garden, enjoying the sun which had scorched up yesterday's rain. Dee crawled around on a rug at their feet, Joe was in his sandpit. They could see him at the end of the garden in his blue bathing trunks and peaked white cap, feverishly digging a trench.

'I want to hear all about the dance,' said Peg when she had brought Kit up to date with all the news about her Surrey trip. She had enjoyed seeing her parents, but today she was feeling jaded; all she really wanted to do was flop.

'It was a good dance, and several people commented on my dress,' Kit began guardedly,

'Including Hugh, I hope?'

'Yes, he liked it.' She was going to have to tell Peg about Hugh, she supposed. She took off her sun-specs and folded them, rehearsing what she would say.

'Was Charles there with Faith?'

Kit's heart bounced in her chest. Peg's questions had the effect of heavy feet on tender places . . . not that she knew that, of course. 'They were both there, and they asked how you were.' She forced a smile into her voice. Peg was lying full length on the grass, a newspaper over her face.

'I heard you and Hugh come in,' she said. 'He didn't stay very long.'

'I didn't especially want him to, Peg.' Kit breathed deeply and said: 'Look, I might as well tell you, and then you'll know . . . I don't think Hugh will be asking me to go out with him again.'

'You've *never* had a row?' Peg jerked upright, flinging the newspaper down.

'No, we've not had a row, we were very civilised. It was just that when we got back, he hinted at marriage, and I had to make it very plain to him that I don't want to remarry, that it's not in my . . . my scheme of things. He was perfectly all right about it, it was all done . . . well, behind glass. He didn't come right out and propose, you see, so I didn't have to refuse him, just make my views clear, but even so it was awful . . . really embarrassing, and painful too. He went soon afterwards.'

'You're mad to turn down a chance like that!' Peg flared explosively. 'Do you realise what a wonderful life you could have had as his wife? Do you realise what he was offering you—the utmost security, every comfort, the best start for Dee. He thinks the world of you, I've always known that. He's so personable, and so nice. I'd *banked* on him asking you to marry him . . . he's right for you . . . can't you see that?'

'I don't love him,' said Kit doggedly.

'I think you do!'

'I don't love him at all!'

'Not in the way you loved Tim, you mean. Well, a fat lot of good that did. You never knew where he was half the time, and when you did he was . . . hopeless!'

'He was nothing of the kind. You never liked him!' Both girls' tempers were rising.

'Too right, I did not. I didn't like what he did to you. You were always on tenterhooks, anxious about him. Harriet spoiled him rotten. He expected you to give in to him in the same way that she did. Bob and I had such high hopes of you ending up with Hugh, living in his house at Cawnford . . .'

'And moving out of here, and selling this house, because that's what it would have meant. You ought to be pleased I'm staying unmarried . . . that way you still have your home.' Too much was being said—oh, too much. Shut up, don't say any more!

'We want to move out, anyway.' Peg glared back at her. 'We want a house of our own, a proper one—Bob can afford it now. We don't want to be stuck at the top of a Victorian pile for ever and ever!'

'Well, don't stay to oblige me!' Kit was as angry as she. 'Move out when you like, I'll find a new tenant, and Dee can be minded in the hospital crêche, which is what I wanted to arrange in the first place. I never wanted to burden you with another child to look after!'

'You're so determined to be independent!' Peg turned her head away.

'I can't help the way I am . . .' Kit began, then

stopped as Peg turned round, and she saw her face. 'Peg, whatever . . . ?'

'Oh, Kit, I'm pregnant again, and I feel so lousy, I feel so rotten. Oh, Kit, I'm so *sorry*!' Peg burst into tears and buried her head in Kit's lap.

Kit hugged her and cradled her, Dee howled in sympathy. Joe looked up from his digging and decided to leave well alone.

The two girls made up their quarrel, but later, when Bob came home, a round-table family conference was held, for issues had been raised, albeit in anger, which had to be sorted out. Naturally enough the Carltons wanted a house once again, especially now that a new baby was expected in early March. 'We're delighted, of course,' Bob said gloomily, 'but we may not be going for ages, and when we do you'll have no trouble . . . in letting again, I mean.' Kit's forced expression of brightness bothered him a lot. She was no doubt wondering who she would get, and what they would be like. And it wouldn't pay her to sell up, either, not with the size of her mortgage. Now, if she was in the commuter zone, with house prices rocketing, it might be a different story. Bob's mind worked, and thrived, and grew on figures . . . he dreamed of them at night. 'You took us in when we needed help most,' he said to Kit on Sunday, as he mowed the lawn and she cut the edges, and Peg in a lighthearted mood washed all her dusters and hung them out on the line. 'But speaking for myself, I'm glad you're not marrying MacBride . . . not that there's anything wrong with him, but he could be a bit of a nag, and I think that in time you'd resent that, Kit.' He bent down and removed a stone from the path of the mower and flung it on one side.

So, once more, peace reigned between the two families at Hilldown, but things weren't quite the same, not so far as Kit was concerned. Bob and Peg would be moving out at some time in the near future. They wanted to move out, and however natural and practical this was, it was also just a shade hurtful, for how long had they been thinking of the upstairs flat as some sort of stopgap, and longing to get away? Peg had called it a 'Victorian pile' and that might be how she viewed it, for things said in anger often hold grains of truth. Things were different —not damaged, but spoiled, and Kit was aware of the change. She felt very alone indeed that weekend, and then when she got to the hospital on Monday morning, trouble awaited her.

'There's been a complaint,' said Sister, 'against you personally.' She had asked Kit to stay behind after assigning the nurses their jobs.

'What kind of complaint?' What on earth had she done, or not done? Kit felt alarmed, but not unduly so, at first. It couldn't be anything much, surely, could it? Yet Sister's face was grave.

'Mr Kelland,' she began in frigid tones, 'was in ICU yesterday, but he came up here afterwards to report that he'd heard you discussing details of his wife's illness on the bus on Friday night. He said he was sitting two seats behind you, and heard every word you said . . . about her having had extensive surgery, about you specialling her, and how, when you were off duty, she had had a serious relapse. He said you implied that the Ward Sister who looked after her in your absence hadn't troubled to supervise her enough . . . meaning me, of course.'

'But Sister . . .' Kit couldn't believe, couldn't credit what she was hearing.

'He said there were several people on the bus who must have heard what he did . . . local people, who knew his family. He said it was a disgrace. He wants the matter laid before the Senior Nursing Officer.'

'But, Sister . . .'

'Naturally, before I do that I would like your side of the story.'

'But Sister, there isn't one! It's not true . . . it's lies!' Kit's voice throbbed with shock. She went deathly pale, while her eyes flashed fire. 'He's made the whole thing up!'

Someone came in; she heard the movement, saw a blur of white coat. It was Charles. He had knocked, but got no answer, and when he opened the door the atmosphere in the cluttered room hit him like a charge. He saw Kit and Sister sitting there as though they were glued in space. Sister's, 'I won't be a minute, Mr Niall,' fell on deaf ears, and purposely deaf, he closed the door and sat down. Kit transferred her gaze to him.

'Mr Niall,' she burst out, 'Walter Kelland has trumped up the most ridiculous story!'

He blinked. 'What kind of story?'

'Leave this to me,' Sister said, but in actual fact she wasn't all that sorry to see Charles Niall there. She was more upset than she cared to admit about Walter Kelland's statement. So instead of reminding Charles that nursing staff problems were hers alone, she explained what had happened, then questioned Kit again. 'Were you on the nine-thirty bus from here on Friday night?'

'Yes, I was,' Kit admitted readily. 'I hadn't got my car.' Her voice tailed off as she remembered that Charles had offered her a lift. If only, if only she had taken it, none of this would have happened. He was looking at her consideringly, his chin was slightly raised, his eyes held a faint look of bafflement. Surely he couldn't think that she would chatter indiscreetly like that on a bus, or anywhere else. It was then, with a bolt of pure horror, that she remembered she had told him she was meeting someone on the bus that night, so what was he thinking now—that she *had* met someone, and had chattered to them, as Kelland had alleged? Oh, he couldn't be . . . he just couldn't be! The palms of her hands were wet.

'Did you talk to anyone on the bus . . . about anything at all?' Sister's questions were going on.

'No, I didn't. I didn't even see anyone, not to consciously notice them. I spoke to no one. It was a miserable evening, I just wanted to get home.' She was talking wildly, and not convincingly, stumbling over her words. She was aware with all her senses of Charles sitting there in judgment. Perhaps it was fortunate for her state of mind that his bleeper began to signal.

'I'll use the phone outside,' he said curtly. She felt the draught from the door as he opened it, passed through, and snapped it shut.

'Is there any reason why Kelland should want to land you in trouble?' Sister went to stand by the window; the sun made a band on her dress. 'In other words, is he trying to get back at you for something you've done to him?'

'Yes, I think that's what it must be.' Kit drew a calming breath. She was fighting back now, and why not . . . why not, for goodness' sake? She had nothing to hide, she could tell the truth, and if the Kelland man persisted in his blatant lies she would rout him out and tackle him. 'He made a pass at me in the waiting-room last week,' she explained. 'It was impossible to fend him off without speaking very plainly. He didn't like it, and if looks could have killed . . .'

'When *was* this?' Sister leaned forward with her palms on the desk.

'Last Wednesday teatime—he came late for visiting, and the physiotherapist was with his wife. I went to the waiting-room to ask him to hang on for a time.'

'Of course—yes, I remember that!' Sister straightened up. 'I saw him myself afterwards, I thought his manner was odd. He reeked of whisky and I thought he'd probably had a good business lunch, a long one, which might have been why he was late.'

'Do you believe my side of the story?'

'Yes, Staff, I do. I know you've not been with us long, but you don't strike me as being an indiscreet chatterer, and I can't quite believe that you'd talk against me . . . at least not in public . . . at least not seriously.'

'I'm not, and I wouldn't,' said Kit. 'But what will happen now?'

'I shall have to tell the SNO, and I'm sure she'll want to see you, but I shall tell her what *I* think, and I'll put my views over strongly. The thing is, however innocent you are, it's your word against Kelland's . . . drat the man!' Sister bit her lip.

'But can't we get hold of him when he comes here, and thrash the whole thing out?'

'He's not likely to admit to having made a pass at you, when his wife was lying ill. He'll say you made that up, in the same way that you'll say he made up *his* piece. I shall have to see what the SNO says, and in the meantime, we'd better get on with what matters most—the care of our patients. You've not met Mrs Valdim, have you? She's due in theatre at ten, so I'll leave her preparation to you, and her pre-medication jab. The peptic ulcer, Mrs Fyne, is fifth on Niall's list, so she'll be going down after lunch, round about two o'clock. Shirley Dixon, the nephrectomy, can have her tube removed. Later this afternoon perhaps you could help me check the drugs. Thank you, that's all, Staff.' She reached for her phone, and Kit went out to start her nursing day.

Miss Jevons, the SNO, whom she saw just before lunch, questioned her with thoroughness, then concluded by saying that she believed her story, even said she was sorry she had been subjected to so much unpleasantness. Kit asked the same question that she had of Sister:

'But what will happen now?'

'At a guess, I would say nothing.' Miss Jevons replaced the top on her pen and leaned back in her chair. 'I doubt if Mr Kelland will come here screaming for blood.

I imagine that all he set out to do was cause aggro for you,' she smiled as she savoured the slang expression. 'I hope he hasn't succeeded.'

Kit shook her head and said he hadn't, yet during the next few days she fancied that relations weren't quite so easy between herself and Sister Clive. It was the same picture as at Hilldown, and as difficult to pinpoint . . . things weren't the same, they seemed irretrievably spoiled. As for Charles, she was quite sure he believed Kelland's story. He probably wouldn't say so to Sister, or anyone else for that matter, but his manner towards her wasn't just remote, it was positively frigid, the hard-flint look in his eyes was always there.

'He's out of his mind with worry over May Kelland,' said Dick Parker, 'she's still on the critical list, doesn't seem to improve.'

'Well, that's not his fault, is it?' They were talking in the office; Dick had just finished his morning round.

'I'm not so sure. Actually, Kit, I can tell you this in confidence. The Prof advised against radical surgery where Mrs K. was concerned. Bearing in mind her weakened state he suggested intubation—in other words, no surgery, just the passing of a tube to make a clear passageway for food.'

'But Dick,' Kit stared, 'in her case, it wouldn't have lasted long . . . it would only have afforded temporary relief!'

'Yes, we all knew that, but the Professor still thought it best to extend her life for a few months, rather than risk an abrupt end to it by putting her through extensive surgery. After hours of talk, surprising though it was, he gave in under pressure. Charles Niall can be very convincing when he thinks his way is right. But now that May Kelland is going downhill, he must be feeling bad, and the Prof isn't above putting the boot in, you know.'

'How terrible for him!'

'Not to mention her!' Dick made his way to Kilross

Ward, wondering why it was that Kit Tennant, with her touch-me-not air, practically always defended Charles Niall. Perhaps she fancied him.

On Friday morning the news came through that May Kelland would recover. She was transferred to the Cardiac Unit, and if her progress continued she would be back in Bellingham Ward in a few days' time.

There was a noticeable change in Charles when he came to do the round. Sister accompanied him, and Kit had no direct contact with him that morning, but surreptitious glances at him, as she sat at the ward desk, showed his mouth turning up at the corners, instead of being gripped straight. Even his thick brows looked reposed, lying above his eyes loose and free, not knitted across his nose. So at least something was going right for someone. Kit lowered her eyes to her charts. And if May Kelland came back to the ward, and if her husband came to see her, she, Kit Tennant, was going to have a few words to say to him. Even thinking about him, and what he had said, still made her blood boil. Why should he be allowed to get away with it?

Walter Kelland was coming away from the west wing—the Thoracic and Cardiac Unit—that afternoon at five o'clock, as Kit crossed the yard to her car. She had just unlocked its door and was climbing inside when she saw him, strutting along in his blazer. She shot after him. He was some way ahead, there were two or three people between her and him. She didn't yell at him to stop, even she baulked at that, but she cried out loud as she felt her arm gripped, as she felt herself being pulled round in a half-circle, and came face to face with Charles. She fought against him, pulled against him. 'Let me go . . . let me go . . . let me *go*! I'm going to have it out with . . .'

'And I say you are not! You are not, do you hear? I forbid it!' His voice was like a stake driving into the heat of her anger, easing it, forcing it out. If he'd shouted at her, shaken her, pulled her, she would have fought him all the more, but his quiet voice, coming as it had, firmly and *sensibly*, brought sweeps of relief, and reason, and thankfulness, flying back. He had stopped her from making a fool of herself, from provoking an ugly scene. He had forced his will on her, and she liked it. He was bossy and autocratic, and she liked that too. She must be out of her mind.

'I must be out of my mind,' she said out loud, and heard him say:

'It's understandable that you want to wring the truth out of him, but short of thumbscrew methods, you wouldn't have any success.' Charles was walking her back to her car with his hand under her arm, using no force; her arm was bare and his touch was a fine magic. I love him, she thought, and I've loved him for a long time, since losing Joe at the Show, and probably long before that; she forgot Walter Kelland, who had long since passed through the hospital gates. 'The best thing to do with a man like him,' Charles was saying at her side, 'is to treat him with the contempt he deserves.' He opened her car door. She propped it wide, but didn't get in, for she didn't want to leave him, nor move away from him, not by so much as an inch.

'You believed me, didn't you?' She smiled at him, letting down her guard.

'I never doubted your story, Kit, not for a single moment.' His eyes were soft yet purposeful, he was looking kisses at her. There was a second when she felt that in spite of the wall of windows at their backs, he might have stepped forward and drawn her close, and covered her mouth with his. She didn't move, but he did, he stepped backwards and she felt his restraint or rejection, like a wave of ice water being flung into her face. 'I must let you get home.'

'How true,' she said. 'I'm in a hurry, as usual.' She dipped at the knees and got into the car, but before she could close the door, Charles peered in at her under the roof.

'By the way, you didn't have to invent a friend on the bus that night to get out of accepting a lift from me—an emphatic 'no' would have done. There was no need to spare my feelings, I'm not a sensitive plant!' He was laughing now, laughing *at* her; all her defences rushed back.

'Perhaps you should be relieved that I'm not dying to be in your company—bearing in mind your half-baked theory about young widows!' she flashed.

She never knew if he answered her, she was too busy starting the car, but a quick glance in her mirror showed him still standing there on the tarmac, as she reached the gates. She gave a loud blare on her horn.

CHAPTER TEN

KIT's hours were altered during the following week. She was rostered to do the night shift on Thursday, and she went on duty at nine-thirty in the evening, which felt very strange indeed. To go to work in twilight was something she hadn't done for a long time, and never at the General, but as soon as she entered the building, all her recollections of past night shifts returned. There was an echoey feeling in the lift, there were fewer staff around, the brightly lit corridors showed gleaming floors, the ward lights were dimmed, and the nurses didn't chatter—or at least, not quite so much.

Sister Clive, at the end of her day shift, went through the report with Kit. The rest of the day staff had gone home, and tonight the ward would be manned by Kit and a student nurse, visited at intervals by the Night Superintendent, Sister Roker, who covered all the wards. 'She comes round about eleven the first time,' said Nurse Linton when they were alone, 'then at one-thirty, and once more round about five o'clock. I usually go up for my meal at one.'

'All right then, stick to that,' Kit agreed, reaching for her torch. She entered the ward and did her round, checking especially the newly op patients, to make sure they were comfortable. She shaded the torch away from their faces, checked intravenous drips, had a whispered word with a new admission—a young Indian girl, who spoke little English and was terrified of the shadows in the ward. Kit drew the curtains round her bed and gave her a night-light; her huge dark eyes expressed her thanks.

Mrs Ava Valdim was in the next bed. She had been moved out of the side-ward to make room for Mrs Kelland who, at teatime that day, had been transferred back to the surgical floor. She was awake, Kit saw. She bent down to her. 'Can't you sleep, Mrs Valdim?' she asked.

'I will soon, dear, I feel all right. It's just strange being in here with so many other people, but it's only for one night. I'm going home tomorrow, as you know. I can hardly believe it's all over.'

Mrs Valdim had made a good recovery from her operation. Without the pressure of her large spleen she could breathe more easily. She no longer felt she was pushing against an immovable object. 'It's a little like when you've given birth,' she had told an amused Charles Niall. 'You feel empty and light, and wonder what's wrong with you!'

Kit hadn't seen Charles since their encounter in the yard, and it was with mixed feelings that she learned he was the surgeon on call tonight. She longed to see him, yet dreaded doing so; she couldn't relax in his presence, nor dare to do so, in case she showed what she felt. It was because of this that she thought she might ask for a transfer to another ward, after her holiday, which was coming up next week. Large hospitals, like large towns, had a swallowing-up capacity. If she was transferred to another block or wing, the chances of running into any of the medical staff on Bellingham were very slim indeed. She intended to give it careful thought; it might be the best thing to do. To be in love with a man who held his views and who, in any case, was plainly involved with the unencumbered and, yes, likeable Faith Melville, was setting herself up like a skittle, and asking to be mown down. And apart from Faith, Kit didn't want to be in love again. It was too enslaving, too demanding, too 'stripping-of-her-will'. She could step back now and not feel too much, she could take herself out of the danger zone without too much heartache. She had *got to do it now*.

After she had finished her round of the main ward she went to side-ward one, pushing the door open quietly and keeping her torch well down. May Kelland was wide awake, however. 'I've been waiting for you,' she smiled. 'It's lovely to see you again, Nurse.'

'And to see you,' replied Kit. She had read Charles's written comments in Mrs Kelland's notes: 'Apart from her improved clinical condition, this patient's morale has improved. The signs of apathy and depression she was showing have taken themselves off. She now talks optimistically of the future, and looks forward to going home.'

'Can you spare a few minutes to talk to me, dear?' she asked, as Kit re-set her pillows.

'We-ell,' Kit smiled at her, 'you should be asleep, you know. Night Sister will be round pretty soon, but still, all right.' Disobeying all rules, she sat down on the bed.

'It's just that I wanted to tell you that my husband and I are separating. He won't be coming in any more, he's got a job abroad. I thought you might think it funny if you didn't see him again.'

'Funny' wasn't quite the word Kit would have used in the circumstances. She was glad he wouldn't be coming in, but that wasn't the right line to take. What she must do was commiserate with May, she must say the conventional things, but before she could start, Mrs Kelland spoke again. 'We've been having a difficult time for ages, and I kept on getting upset. I hate arguments, and we were even having them when he came to visit me here. But now he's going to Spain, and we shan't live together again. He told me last Friday when he came to see me down in the Cardiac Ward. I was feeling so much better that day, so was able to take it in. And do you know, I'm almost ashamed to have to admit it, but all I felt when he left me was relief.'

'These things happen, Mrs Kelland.' Kit knew she must guard her tongue. It wouldn't do, for instance, to tell May she was well rid of her husband.

'The best thing is that *he's* leaving *me*, and not the other way round. He could have been difficult if I'd made the break. Men are rather like that, you know.'

Were they indeed? Kit made herself smile and agree with her on the surface. 'Now you must get some sleep,' she added, 'but I'm very glad you've told me.' Leaving the door ajar, she went out into the corridor. Patients' marital problems were something no nurse should air her views on. Kit hoped she had been noncommittal enough, without sounding unsympathetic. But inside she seethed . . . what a louse Walter Kelland was!

The second of the two side-wards was empty, and Kit glanced in as she passed. She was just about to go into the office when she heard the distant thud of the corridor doors, followed by a heavy plodding and rustling. Night Sister Roker, for sure, and yes, there she was, big and broad with greying hair, a dress that was starched too stiffly, broad feet planted at ten to two. A torch like a truncheon swung from her belt, steel-rimmed glasses bounced on her bust, secured by a chain round her neck. 'You're new!' she accused, staring at Kit.

'No, Sister, I've been here since May, but this is my first time on nights.'

'*And* you've got a free bed,' once again Sister accused.

Kit admitted she had. It was like confessing to a mortal sin. What a terror Sister was!

'Then make it up and send it down to number one theatre. An accident case has just been admitted. A young woman has been injured by a youth stunting on a BMX bike on the pavement near Elvin Bridge. The girl was on foot, coming home from a dance; she crawled here on all fours, collapsed outside the porter's lodge, with internal injuries. She'll go into Recovery from Theatre, of course, so you've plenty of time to prepare.'

'What a shocking thing!' Kit felt she had to make some kind of comment.

'The world is full of shocking things, Staff Nurse.' Sister peered at her more closely. 'Weren't you a patient here, not long ago?'

'Yes, Sister, in June. I had appendicitis.'

'So you did. I remember . . . never forget a face.' Sister had a good look at all the patients' faces in the ward, snorted at the childish night-light by the Indian girl's bed. 'You're soft, Nurse Tennant, but never mind, it's not a bad fault to have, not even for a nurse, providing it's kept in reasonable check.' She plodded and rustled back down the corridor and out to Kilross Ward. Kit asked Nurse Linton to make up the theatre bed.

'Can I still go for my meal at one?' Nurse Linton was always hungry.

Kit told her she could. 'And bring something back for me, will you, Nurse? I'd better not leave the floor, not with this new patient coming. Something cold will do —salad and cheese, or something like that. Because I couldn't, in any case, she thought, cope with a full roast dinner at one o'clock in the morning. My inside might be good, but it's not tuned in to night duty yet.'

The night wore on, and the luminous hands of the big ward clock indicated two-fifteen when the staff nurse from Recovery rang through to say that Linda Clease was on her way up. 'She has a crushed abdomen, ruptured colon, diffuse peritonitis. Her notes and charts and treatment sheet are coming up with the porters. Is everything all right at your end?'

'Yes, fine, we're ready for her.' Ten minutes later Linda Clease was wheeled into side-ward two.

She was young, with long dark hair tied back in a piece of crêpe bandage. She was pale and drowsy, and doll-like, lying against her pillows in a sitting position, with a drip running into her arm. A gastric tube was taped to her cheek, she was on quarter-hourly obs. And she might, Kit knew, need oxygen, if the distention in her abdomen grew any worse and caused breathing difficulties.

'You're in a side-room on Bellingham Ward,' said Kit, close to her face. 'You'll be with us now till you're quite better, there's nothing to worry about.'

'Mum and Dad?' Linda's eyes opened wide and tried to focus on Kit.

'Casualty has let them know what happened. They'll be able to see you tomorrow.'

'I'm thirsty . . . can I have a drink?'

'Only little sips, I'm afraid. We need to rest your tummy for a time.' Kit held a feeding cup to the girl's lips, making sure that only drips entered her mouth. Then sitting down by the bed she read the medication sheet. She was to have pethidine to keep her pain-free, reinforced with phenobarbitone. Her antibiotic—to control the peritoneal infection—was to be administered through the intravenous drip.

Charles Niall had done his part, the patient's recovery now would depend on skilled and vigilant nursing; but Linda Clease had youth on her side, which must count for something. Leaving Nurse Linton at her side, Kit went to the main ward to make sure all was well there.

Sister Roker paid her second visit, looked in on the new patient, asked to see her charts, and remarked that poor Mr Niall had had to deal with two other emergencies since midnight. 'There was a coach crash on the motorway, three serious cases, two of them were sent here. Don't look so anxious, Nurse . . . one was a gynae case, so she went into Abbott Ward, and the other, an elderly man, was admitted to Kilross with pelvic injuries. Mr Niall picked the wrong night!'

'I hope he'll be able to rest before he starts tomorrow's list, or rather, today's list,' said Kit, looking at the clock.

'Surgeons have their own methods of keeping going,'

said Sister. 'It's part of their training . . . like the Army, you know . . . all those assault courses, and endurance tests, and things like that. They stand them in good stead.'

Kit watched her go plopping off again, but she couldn't for the life of her imagine how a soldier's training could compare with a surgeon's. Hadn't Sister got rather mixed up? It was such a far-flung similarity that she burst out laughing. Well, at least there was always something to have a giggle about. Hospital life had its funny side as well as its grim one, which was just as well, or the staff would all go mad.

Linda Clease's temperature had risen to 39°C, with a correspondingly raised pulse rate, when Kit did her observations at four. In the end, therefore, she was relieved to see Charles's head come round the door. If he was surprised to see her he gave no sign, her quiet 'Good morning' was answered with a nod as he took the charts from her hand. He was in slacks and sweater, his hair was rumpled, he looked as though he had changed in a great hurry from his theatre clothes. He looked far more approachable without his white coat, his hands smelled of hibiscrub.

'Her observations aren't unduly alarming,' he told Kit in the office, 'but if her temperature climbs any higher I'm afraid we have to assume that we aren't controlling the infection adequately enough. It may be necessary to increase her antibiotic dose. The next thirty-six hours will give us a clearer picture. In the meantime,' he passed a hand wearily over his head, 'her condition is much as I expected.' He yawned and apologised.

'I hear you've had quite a night of it.' As she spoke Kit could hear the rattle of cups and the tinkle of spoons. Nurse Linton and she were hoping to have a cup of tea before Sister's Roker's third visit round about five o'clock.

'Yes,' said Charles, and looked up at her, out of

red-rimmed eyes, 'can I have some tea, please?'

'Why, yes,' she said, 'of course you can. I'm sorry I didn't offer, but I thought . . . I assumed . . . you'd have had some down in theatre block.'

'I did, but I'm still as dry as a husk.' He sounded it too, his voice has a rasp. Kit turned to the door.

'We'll soon cure that.'

'Can you break for ten minutes and have some with me?'

'I think that could be arranged!' They smiled at one another, and the thought sprang into Kit's mind that loving a man had so many facets, and plain, ordinary caring was one of them. She sped to the kitchen on wings.

When she came back with tea and biscuits Charles had opened the office window which led out on to a tiny balcony, giving a near view of the bicycle sheds and the hospital laundry, while farther towards the east, the long, swooping line of the Downs stood out sharp and clear as the sun rose, streaking them with light.

'A sight for sore eyes.' He fetched two chairs and placed them side by side.

'I can never decide what colour the Downs really are,' replied Kit. 'They can look green or gold, purple or brown, and at times nearly black. They'd drive an artist mad, wouldn't they, trying to mix the right shade?'

He nodded, enjoying his tea. 'Does Faith paint?' asked Kit.

'She dabbles, yes.' His answer was short, and she got the firm impression that he had something on his mind that he wanted to talk about. What was it? she wondered. She waited for him to start.

The dawn air was chilly, and seeing her hug herself, Charles stepped back into the office, and hooked a cloak off the back of a chair. 'It's Sister Clive's,' she told him, as he put it round her shoulders.

'She'd not grudge you the loan of it, I'm sure.' He sat down again, then asked her if she had seen May Kelland.

'For a few minutes, yes, and considering what she's been through she looked—well, pretty good.' She caught his eye, or he caught hers.

'So you know her husband's gone off?' he asked.

'As you do, obviously.'

'Her sister told me today. They're going to live together, the sister is a retired nurse, she's selling her flat in Northumberland and they're buying a place together. I'm glad for May Kelland's sake.'

'I know . . . that's how I feel. She's due for some happiness. I know one shouldn't feel pleased when married couples split up, but even so . . .'

'As you say, even so.' Charles stared at her thoughtfully.

'Walter Kelland scared me rigid,' Kit confessed.

'Now that I *don't* believe! Little does he know that I saved him from going off to Spain with two black eyes, after fisticuffs with a certain young staff nurse, who can probably pack quite a punch when she's roused; she's got the right colour hair!'

'It's not quite red, and I wouldn't have struck him!' Kit laughed, enjoying the joke, but Charles's face quickly sobered; he had something else to tell her. 'You remember the Benticks, don't you?' he asked.

'Why yes, of course I do. Mrs Bentick was here the first week I started. She and her husband had a greengrocery business . . . still have, I expect. I remember you carrying her case for her that afternoon she went home. You warned her about lifting crates—she'd had a hernia. They were the couple who were so devoted.' She smiled as she remembered the plump and lumbering Mr Bentick all but running to meet his wife. But Charles's silence alerted her. 'What's happened to them?' Her question came sharply; she turned round on the chair.

'John Bentick had a brain haemorrhage, he died here at the General a fornight ago. He lived only three days, never came out of the coma.'

'Oh, how awful . . . poor Mrs Bentick!'

'Yes, it's a wretched business,' Charles agreed. 'I only heard about it tonight, down in A & E. There are times when news in this building travels like a dart, and times, like this one, when it seems to get stuck. I would like to have seen Alice Bentick.'

'I wonder how she'll manage,' said Kit. 'Perhaps she'll sell the business. It wouldn't be easy for her to run it, unless she had loads of help.' She shifted inside the borrowed cape, its collar bulged out her hair, 'Isn't life extraordinary, when you come to think about it? On the one hand you get a couple parting because they can't get on, and then you hear of a devoted pair, forced and wrested apart by the most final of all . . . occurrences.'

'Yes, I know.' She saw him nod, but he said nothing more than that. There was no need, and neither was there the slightest friction between them, just a friendly silence that had peace in it, a silence that was presently broken by morning sounds. Kit came to with a jolt. There was the first car, the first bus, the barking of a dog, the hollow clomping of a night watchman's boots as he went home to breakfast. Soon the morning rush would begin inside the hospital wards—temperatures, pulses, teas, wash-bowls, medicines to give out. Down in the yard she could see Sister Roker crossing over from Milton Wing. That meant she would be on the surgical floor in roughly four minutes . . . the time it took to boil an egg.

'That's my cue to go back in,' she said to Charles, who followed her glance.

'Mine too, I guess.' He got up and joined her at the rail. 'I would like to see Linda Clease again before I leave the ward.'

The night was over, the day had begun. He turned

round and picked up the chairs. They both went in, and with the clicking to of the balcony windows, the quiet time they had shared was shut outside.

Kit spent most of Friday catching up on her sleep, but on Saturday afternoon she decided to walk into the town to see if Mrs Bentick was at her shop. She felt she wanted to see her to say how sorry she was about her husband, and also to ask how she was.

It was warm again, in fact, it was hot, a typical late August day. Kit changed her jeans for a cotton dress with a low frilled neckline, loose elbow-length sleeves and a narrow belt. It was vivid emerald, it suited her hair, and she turned a number of heads, male and female, as she walked along in the sun.

Mrs Bentick's shop was in Garth Road, leading off the High Street. Kit got there just after four-thirty, a time when the shopping crowds were beginning to thin and turn to the cafés for tea. And Alice was in the shop and serving; there was a young boy helping her. As she reached up for some bananas in the window she saw Kit standing outside. Her face broke into a wide smile, she beckoned and mouthed 'Come in'.

'Go right through to the back, dear,' she said, as Kit walked into the shop. 'I'll be with you in a jiffy, there's a friend of yours in there.' So perhaps Kit shouldn't really have been as surprised as she was to see Charles in there, sitting on a chair that had no back, and looking for him, tidy and well pressed, in slacks and shirt with a neatly knotted tie.

'Two great minds think alike,' he said, unrolling himself, standing straight and tall by a wall of crates that had green leaves sticking through. 'I must admit I wondered, though, if you'd try to see Mrs Bentick.'

'Well, I never dreamed you would!' The surpise of seeing him there jettisoned her sharp retort which, even to her, sounded rude.

'I probably have a few humanitarian instincts,' he

said. He gave her his chair and remained standing leaning against the crates.

'I'm sorry, I didn't mean . . .' began Kit, just as Alice Bentick came in. She was pleased to see them, but apologised for showing them into her stockroom.

'How are you managing?' Charles sasked her.

'Oh, all right, sir, I think. I have a boy to help me, and he can drive the van. He's my neighbour's son, in Elton Street, he was looking for a job. Then I have an odd job man—the pot-man, as John used to call him; he does all the lifting and lumping and humping about.'

'I'm afraid we didn't hear about your husband until yesterday,' said Kit, getting up and offering Alice her chair.

'He was a good man.' She wouldn't sit down, in case she had to hurry out to serve in the shop; she kept her eye on the door. 'We'd been married nearly forty years, we'd have had our anniversary, our ruby one, on the fifteenth of next month. It happened in the night, you know, that haemorrhage in his head. They called it a CVA at the hospital.' She glanced at Charles for confirmation, and Kit saw him give a nod. 'He was in hospital three days and two nights, but he never came out of the coma. Still, he didn't know anything, nor suffer any pain.' She stopped for a second or two, remembering, then she looked across at Kit. 'I saw you one night, dear, when I'd been to visit him. It was on the bus. I spoke to you, but you were that wrapped up in thought, sitting there all quiet like, that I don't think you saw me, did you? You looked away out of the window, and I couldn't attract your attention. It was after nine o'clock at night, on the bus from the hospital.'

A pulse fluttered in Kit's throat. 'No, I didn't see you,' she said, 'but I know when it was, though, the night my car was in dock.' And it was *that* night . . . *that* night . . . was all she could think, for the moment. It was the night when someone else saw me—Walter Snake Kelland, with his flat head and his forked tongue, dripping poison into my life, and suspicion into other people's minds. She heard Charles get to his feet.

'I offered her a lift that night, but she turned me down flat,' he said, sounding rueful on purpose, trying to make them laugh. He succeeded with Alice Bentick.

'Well, you know what they say, Mr Niall . . . if at first you don't succeed, try, try again! Now, it looks as though *I* must try again, for I see there's a queue in my shop.' She bustled out, squeezing between two sacks.

'So now you know I was speaking the truth!' Kit was flushed with excitement. Charles nodded. He appeared unmoved.

'I never doubted your word, my dear, it didn't have to be proved, but if you're glad . . . well, that's fine.'

'Wouldn't you be?' she flashed.

He considered that, then smiled at her. 'Yes, I think I know how you feel. I shall certainly mention it to Sister—just in passing, of course. And knowing her, I quite expect that, also in passing, she will in due course inform the SNO.'

'Oh, Charles, thank you!'

'Don't mention it!' He lifted her up from the chair. His arms slipped round her, tightened and held her, so close she could scarcely breathe. His warm length lay against hers, her head was on his shoulder. She could feel his heart, or was it her own, thundering in her ears. When he moved she raised her face for his kiss and latched her arms round his neck. There was just a second when she saw his mouth, long, firm and unsmiling, before it met hers, and moulded to hers, softly brushing and seeking, then firmly insistent, drawing the strength from her limbs. Don't let it, don't let it . . . don't let it end . . . clamoured in her brain, but of course it did, and back came the stockroom with its crates and boxes and sacks. From outside came the call of the newsboy, and from close against her ear, came Charles's voice, as he moved away from her.

'Now that,' he said unevenly, 'could be proof of a different kind.'

Kit remained silent, searching his face, but could glean nothing from it, except that it was no longer mocking; his eyes had a glittery look. 'Perhaps we should go,' she managed to say, hearing the shake in her voice. But once away from him, out of his range, a measure of calm returned. She stooped for her bag and swung it in place. 'Well, *I'm* going if you're not.' Avoiding his eyes, she walked ahead into the shop.

They took their leave of Mrs Bentick, who came out into the street and waved them off, as she blinked away tears, then went back to deal with her queue. 'She's what I would describe as "game".' Charles got into step beside Kit. Once they reached the High Street she expected he would say goodbye and speed away to Faith's shop, only a few yards away. But he made no move towards it, and he seemed in no hurry to go. 'I believe you're on holiday next week?' He slowed down and came to a stop, and so did she.

'Yes, I start on Thursday. I'll be away three weeks. I feel rather badly about it I had all that sick leave in June and July. It's not fair to the other staff.'

'Nonsense!' Charles epostulated. 'That has nothing to do with it. Sick leave is bad luck, a holiday is fun . . . or should be. Look, let's sit down.' He indicated the tables set outside the Creamery Café. 'We might as well take the weight off our feet and have a spot of refreshment.'

'I suppose we might.' It was still going on, this stolen time with him. He wasn't rushing off to Faith, after all; Kit hugged that thought to herself. He did everything so unfussily, and perfectly, she noted as he gave their order—tall glasses of iced fruit juice instead of burning hot tea.

'I shall be at home for the first ten days—my mother-in-law is coming,' she told him. 'She comes quite a lot, actually; she likes to see Dee. Then during the last week I go up to Scotland to visit my parents—they live at Cannoch Moor in the Highlands. My father's the local GP.'

'So you're a Scots lassie, but without the accent!'

'It comes out when I'm fashed.' Kit returned his smile, and immediately felt close to him again. She thought of his kiss, and the feel of his arms, and the latch of his bodily warmth. She had the feeling that he was thinking the same sort of thoughts, and she went on talking to try to dispel the ache of longing inside her. 'I've spent most of my life in the south,' she told him. 'I went to school in Kent—my maternal grandparents lived there then. I spent half-terms with them, then went up to Cannoch Moor for the longer holidays. I did my nursing training in Alverstone, and I married a Kent man. My mother was a southerner, so I suppose you could say I have mixed nationality.'

'An enchanting hybrid!' Charles put down his glass and covered her hand with his. It was cold from the ice in the glass, yet it burned straight through her like a torch.

'You're flirting with me, Mr Niall!' she teased to hide her feelings, while her traitorous hand, with a mind of its own, turned palm up to clasp his own.

'Are you going to marry Hugh MacBride?' he asked.

'Because we're both Scots, you mean?'

'No, not for that reason. You might be in love with the man.'

'I might, yes.' It was no time for banter, she knew that very well. Yet self-protection, a wish even now, to step back from the brink, to step back and not get involved with a man who was plainly in love with someone else, and could turn her world upside down, made her go on and say: 'We've talked about it, because you see, unlike yourself, Hugh doesn't regard a widow with a baby as some kind of predator.'

Charles's face darkened, then paled. He withdrew his hand. 'How fortunate for you that he doesn't.'

And it was then, at that point exactly, that they heard the shattering bang—a whoosh of sound, a dull roar, a rushing and tumbling, like bricks falling . . . and it came from near at hand.

People leapt to their feet, exclaimed, cried out. Someone yelled: 'It's an explosion!' They smelled smoke, and Kit saw the horror on Charles's face as he looked down the street, towards Faith's shop.

'Ring for an ambulance, the fire brigade . . . then stay where you are. It may be dangerous!' he shouted at her.

And then he began to run.

CHAPTER ELEVEN

KIT'S FIRST thought was to follow him, but she went back into the café, dialled 999 and asked for all three services. Then she too, was running, running, running towards Faith's shop.

There was no crowd round the entrance now, which looked much the same as usual. People were massed a short distance away, pointing and shouting! 'It's at the back . . . it's at the back!' Cars were slowing down; a girl on horseback dismounted; someone called out to Kit: 'Keep away, keep away . . . it might not be safe in there!'

But she was in already—choking, coughing, moving through brick-dust and smoke. She crouched down . . . don't breathe . . . don't breathe . . . try to hold your breath. She half ran, half crawled blindly into the back. And there she felt the scorch of flames, and found herself looking through a jagged hole as big as a tunnel mouth. In the yard beyond, on a patch of green, she could just make out the kneeling form of Charles reaching out for Faith. She managed to reach them, scrabbling over debris as the ambulance arrived, followed by a fire engine, followed by the police. The ambulance-men obtained access through the ironmonger's next door. Faith took one look at the stretcher they carried and immediately sat up. She was covered in grime, her hair was down, her dress torn at the waist. 'I'm not going to hospital, so take that thing away!'

'Now look, Faith . . .' Charles's arm was round her.

'You can't make me go!'

But he could, as Kit very well knew, and yet he didn't persist. 'I'm fairly sure she's not injured, just badly shocked' he told the men. 'I'll look after her, keep an eye on her, and if I'm at all unsure, I'll get her along to Casualty at once.'

'Very well, sir.' They knew who he was and respected his judgment. So off they went, disappointing the ghouls, now pushed back by the police, who had cordoned off the area while the fire brigade got to work.

Charles and Faith, with Kit following, were led across the road to the public library, where they were able to wash, where tea was brought to them, and where one of the police officers talked to Faith. She was very upset, Kit could see her legs shaking under her skirt as she sat. One of her hands was tight in Charles's, the other was balled in a fist. Her mouth trembled, but her voice was controlled. There were no histrionics, no attempt at all to mask the facts. 'It was my fault,' she began quietly. 'I knew the boiler was old. I'd never used it before, but today I took a chance. I had so much rubbish to get rid of, and the gardens at the back of the shops are too close to have bonfires, and the dustmen don't always oblige. I prised open the top of the boiler—the weight of *that* nearly creased me! and started it burning with firelighters, then dumped all my stuff on top. I had to be quick, I had customers waiting—Saturdays are always busy. So I banged down the lid and left it . . . it seemed to be all right.

'After a bit I smelt something odd, and I had a horrible feeling that there might have been paint tins amongst all the packing. I panicked a bit then, I think, and I went back with the idea of raking it out. But when I got in there, into the boiler-room, it was just like a furnace. The boiler was red-hot, juddering and roaring. I didn't know what to do. And then it went off . . . there was nothing but noise. I saw the wall blow out, and then I was flying after it, hurtling into the garden. I couldn't feel my legs, and I couldn't scream . . . it was all so quick, so fast. The garden was cold, I remember that, and then I must have fainted. The next thing I knew I was on the grass, and Charles was calling my name.'

'She missed hitting the garden wall by less than a foot.' Charles's look dared the constable to say very much; so getting the message, he merely delivered a homily about blocked flues, and the dangers of boilers which were over fifty years old.

When they went back over the road an hour later, the dust in the shop was settling. It lay like sand on the carpet and shelves, trickled off ornaments, coated pictures, clung to silks and wools. The stench of burning was everywhere, even out in the yard, but the band of men who had come to clear up and make the building safe had done a wonderful job in such a short space of time. The yard had been cleared, so had what remained of the little back room. Scaffolding was being drilled through to support the bedroom above. Boarding would be erected to entirely enclose the back. 'Once you've got your Toby jugs dusted, madam, you'll be able to trade again,' said one of the men, wiping his face with a rag. It wasn't a matter for joking, but as Charles said afterwards, what else was there? They could hardly sit down and weep.

The police advised Faith not to live in the flat till the building had been repaired. 'Downstairs there's no danger, upstairs we can't be sure. Go up and pack a bag by all means. We can help with accommodation . . . that is, if you haven't got . . .'

'Miss Melville will come home with me . . . no problem.' Charles watched Faith with an eagle eye as she made her way upstairs. He wanted to go up with her, Kit could see that.

'If there's nothing I can help with, I'd better get home,' she said.

'Oh, Kit, of course . . . I'm sorry.' He turned round at once. He went to the door with her, the intact shop door, with its inner coating of dust.

'What a good thing the blast went outwards and back, not through here into the street,' she said, letting him open the door; she could feel him looking at her.

'Are you sure you're OK?' She didn't know how tired and drained she looked, nor did she realise that her emerald dress had a two-inch hem of soot.

'Of course I'm all right, I'm not the one who was hurled into outer space.' Her voice was brittle, it had to be, or the look of concern in his eyes—for her at that moment—might have broken her up.

'Please come home with Faith and me . . . we're getting a taxi. Please do that—you look all in.' He closed the door again.

'No, really, Charles . . . I want to walk, I need some fresh air in my lungs,' Kit insisted.

'Then I'll come with you to the corner, get you through all that mob.' Before she could protest again he opened the door, and with an arm about her shoulders, keeping her close to him, and the crowd at bay, he got her to the corner and round to the taxi rank. 'Take this lady to Hilldown, Mount Cliff Road,' he said to the driver of the nearest car, and thrust a note into his hand. After that he walked back to the shop. 'No, it *wasn't* a bomb,' he told several people; then he went inside to Faith.

As Kit didn't see Charles at the hospital on Monday, she decided to stop off in the High Street on her way home, and take a look at Faith's shop. She might even be in it . . . I ought to have rung and enquired about her yesterday, she thought. But somehow or other, ringing Charles's flat, knowing that Faith was there with him, had been something she couldn't quite bring herself to do.

She parked the car, made her way to the shop—and yes, Faith was there. She had no customer and seemed pleased to see Kit, drawing her attention to the spick and span condition of everything in sight. 'Charles and a friend cleaned it up yesterday. I was laid out, I'm afraid . . . reaction, I suppose. I felt ghastly . . . but haven't they done a good job?'

Kit agreed that they had, and as for Faith, she was back to her normal self—eyecatching in a lemon dress, her hair on top of her head, puffed out in the style of a geisha girl. 'I'm in good form,' she said, when Kit enquired, 'in fact, never better.' Kit felt she knew why; she also felt a fool for coming. Why had she bothered? Faith had Charles looking after her. 'Charles hasn't cast one single stone of blame at me,' she said, 'but then that's him all over—he never ever nags. And you know, when I think of what I did, I feel quite sick. Supposing I'd damaged neighbouring properties, people might have been killed.'

Kit couldn't help but agree with her, remembering, as she did so, the look on Bob's face when he was told about the explosion next door to his office. He hadn't been there, it being a Saturday, but as soon as he heard the news, he went off like a shot, to make sure his walls hadn't cracked. Afterwards he had taken the trouble to keep his thoughts to himself, but both Peg and Kit gained the firm impression that Bob's most valued client had gone down in his estimation, several rungs or so. 'Still,' Peg said, 'I expect she's all right, moved in all cosy with Charles. Perhaps she blew up her boiler on purpose . . . the end justifying the means.'

'For heaven's sake, Peg, let it rest!' Bob had protested, as he saw Kit's face.

An account of the explosion was in the paper on Monday night, and on Tuesday half the hospital knew that Mr Charles Niall and Staff Nurse Tennant had been at the scene. The reportage was dramatic, even bordering on the lurid: 'Blast rips out wall at the Craft Shop' . . . 'Proprietor hurled yards' . . . 'Doctor and nurse rush to the scene' . . . 'Blocked boiler flue the cause'.

There was even a photograph of Charles and Faith, laden with cases, getting into a taxi at the kerb.

Kit saw Charles during Tuesday afternoon, when he came to see Linda Clease. 'Good of you to call in on Faith last night. You've had no ill effects of Saturday yourself, I hope?' He raised an enquiring brow.

'None.' There was silence, then:

'Good,' he said. 'Now, are these Miss Clease's notes?' Taking them from her hand before she'd had time to so much as nod, he went into the side-ward, Kit following at his heels. He smiled down at Linda. 'Feeling more yourself, Miss Clease?'

'Yes, thank you,' she smiled back at him. Her parents had been in to see her. There were pink carnations and maidenhead fern in a vase on her locker; get-well cards were strung on her bed-rail, and the utilitarian bandage that had bound back her hair was replaced with a Fergie bow.

'Once her stitches are out she can be started on gentle abdominal exercises,' Charles said in the office. 'Make the arrangements, please. Oh dear,' he gave an impatient flick with his fingers and turned round, 'you're off on Thursday, aren't you . . . starting your holiday?'

'I can make the arrangements before I go. I'll see Physio tomorrow.' Kit scribbled a note on the jotter on the desk.

'I may not see you tomorrow, I've got a full theatre list.'

'Yes, I know you have.' She straightened and smiled, 'So have a good holiday, and come back like a lion refreshed, as my father always says.'

But I shall come back, she thought, as she watched him go, and put in for a transfer—preferably to the ENT Wing, where maybe I can forget you, put you out of my mind and settle down.

* * *

Harriet's train was due in at twelve forty-five on Thursday. Kit put Dee into a scarlet dress with white polka dots, red strapped shoes and a white linen hat with a brim. As they stood at the barrier, watching the people flooding off the train, they spied Harriet in the far distance, wheeling a self-porter trolley. It was piled up like a mountain and she was waving from behind it. She had enough luggage for a month, and Kit felt her spirits sinking. 'Give Granny a wave,' she said to Dee, but the baby disdained to do so; fixing her eye instead on a mangy-looking pigeon, busily pecking crumbs from under a seat.

After that it was greetings, and exclamations, and loading all the luggage into Kit's boot, while Harriet strapped Dee into her seat at the back. 'My lovely little girl . . . and *walking*! You didn't tell me, Kit.'

'I thought we'd surprise you.' Kit closed the boot. 'She's only just started to do it, and she still needs a hand to steady her, otherwise she's down.'

'She's a clever, clever little girl!' Harriet sat in the back with the baby, making Kit feel uncommonly like one of the taxi-drivers, honking their way across the station yard.

Part of Harriet's luggage was presents; she was very generous. There was a joint of boiled bacon, another of beef . . . 'get them in the fridge quickly, dear.' There was homemade jam, a jar of pickles, half a Stilton cheese. There was a new dress for Dee and a coat to go with it, and a brown velvet monkey; a bottle of sherry for Peg and Bob.

The first three days of her visit passed pleasantly enough. They had a picnic in Ashdown Forest, and a day on Barhampton beach. On Sunday Kit cooked one of her speciality lunches. Peg and Bob came down for it . . . it was a happy family occasion. Harriet washed up afterwards, refusing all efforts to help, and disdaining to use the dish-washer. 'You never know what it's doing,' she said, plunging everything into the sink.

It was while she was so engaged that Peg told Kit that she and Bob had found a house, had made an offer for it which had been accepted; she was very excited indeed. 'It's in Furzedown Road, number twenty-eight, three-bedroomed and detached. It's only four years old, so we needn't have very much done. There's a sizeable garden at the back, and there's even a swing. We could be in by late October. Isn't it wonderful!'

Kit agreed that it was, she was glad for them, but inwardly she quailed . . . well, just a little. New people upstairs—what would it be like? She was sure she would get used to it; she must advertise the flat. She might even put a notice on the board in the hospital. She might get a couple of nurses, or other hospital staff, as decent flats were always in demand.

She mentioned the matter of the Carltons' new house to Harriet next day. Her mother-in-law went very quiet, apart from her first outburst of dismay when she thought of the baby, Dee. 'But how will you manage? You can't leave her with strangers. Where is Furzedown Road? Will you be able to take Dee along there for Peg to mind?'

'No, Harriet, I won't; it's on the other side of town. I wouldn't do that, anyway—Peg has done her bit for me. Obviously we'll still help one another out from time to time, but I shan't batten on Peg's good nature, as I'm conscious of doing now.'

'You do plenty for her,' said Harriet, going out into the garden to hang her underclothes, and Dee's cot blanket, out on the line to dry.

She had a long telephone conversation with Alan, her husband, that evening. For this time, on this visit, he wasn't out of the country. Harriet had come to stay because she couldn't keep away. She had left Alan Tennant in the capable hands of her twice-weekly woman, who had promised she would come in every day.

Kit was struck by Harriet's aura of simmering excitement when at last she came back into the room. As she said nothing for a minute or two, she asked how Alan was. 'Oh, he's fine, dear . . . perfectly all right.' Harriet was knitting at speed. 'Now look, dear, I've been thinking, and I've got a suggestion to make. I mentioned it to Alan and he agreed with me at once.' She stabbed her pins into the ball of wool, and gave all her attention to Kit. 'Why don't you give up your job here, and come to live with us? The house is plenty big enough, you could have your own rooms. You could get a job easily at Alverstone Infirmary, your old hospital. I could look after Dee, of course. It would all be so simple. You and Dee are so dear to me,' she added in desperation, for she had seen the refusal in her daughter-in-law's eyes before Kit had time to lower them.

'Oh, Harriet, I'm terribly sorry,' Kit put a hand on her arm, 'but I don't really think an arrangement like that would work out in the long term. It's terribly good of you and Alan, but I must be independent. You see, I *can* manage on my own, and Dee won't suffer, I promise you that—I would give my life for her.'

'So would I, if it came to it.' Harriet was knitting again, even more furiously than before; her fingers had to be busy. 'The offer will never be closed to you, Kit,' she said after a pause. 'If you change your mind, or get into difficulties, you have only to ring us up.'

'I know, Harriet, and thank you,' said Kit unsteadily, getting up to make their bedtime drinks.

The subject wasn't raised again, and all went well until three days later, when Harriet went down with a cold. 'But I never catch colds!' She was annoyed to have to miss her morning jog, but her head ached, and jogging would have been purgatory, she felt. She wouldn't stay in bed, but she did agree to keep indoors and rest. The weather had changed, anyway. Rain-clouds swept the sky, and the wind howled as though it were autumn.

She had a slight cough next day, Wednesday, and on looking down her throat, Kit diagnosed tracheitis. 'You've caught some nasty bug,' she said sympathetically, dosing Harriet up.

Harriet was noticeably better on Thursday, but announced her intention of going back home. 'It's not right to stay, I might give my germs to the baby.' She packed her cases, ignoring Kit's protests.

'But, Harriet, you're still far from right. You might just as well stay till the weekend, as you planned to; another two days will make all the difference.' But Harriet was adamant. 'Well, in that case, I'm driving you.' Kit could be forceful too. 'You're not making that journey by train, you're simply not up to it. Peg will look after Dee, and if we set off after lunch, I can still be back here before dark. It's only two hours each way.' She spoke so firmly that Harriet gave way . . . how lovely to be driven! To get into the car at Kit's gate and out at her own would be effortless. She thanked her daughter-in-law.

The journey was made without event, and shortly after three-thirty, Harriet and Alan Tennant and Kit were all drinking tea in the sitting-room of 10 Dean Road, Alverstone, Kent. Alan Tennant was pleased to see Kit again. 'I'll soon get Harriet right. It was good of you to bring her, Kit,' he looked at her with affection. 'You're prettier than ever, isn't she, Harrie?' And both he and his wife's gaze went to the photograph on the mantelshelf . . . Tim and Kit on their wedding day. Tucked in the frame was a coloured snapshot of Dee.

I ought to go and see them far more than I do, passed through Kit's mind, as she started her journey for home. It was very nearly September, soon the leaves would be turning, but Kit's thoughts turned to her marriage, which sometimes seemed light years away, as though it had happened to someone else. She had married at nineteen, much against her parents' and grandparents' wishes . . . you're both too young . . . Tim won't settle . . . at twenty-five, he's still a boy, a spoiled boy. Kit could hear them now. But she and Tim had married and been happy, and yet . . . and yet . . . she had been disappointed, and knew she had, for Tim, while he strained to give her all the material things which he felt were so important, he never really gave of himself . . . rarely considered her wishes. So it hadn't been easy, but in time . . . given time . . . if Tim hadn't died, it would have got better, they would have made it work; they would have worked at it together.

Who do you think you're kidding? asked the Voice of Truth in her head. Your marriage was mediocre, and it would *never* have got any better. There was love of a kind, but not enough of it; Tim's love for you had no strength. He was weak, anyway, wasn't he? You were always defending him, pulling him out of awkward situations and losing friends in the process. And it's time you put all that behind you, the Voice went remorselessly on. What about Charles? It won't hurt you to think about him, you know. But it did . . . it did. The Voice was wrong, for it did hurt very much. Loving Charles, and thinking about it, was applied and awful anguish. Even if he cared for her, and perhaps he did, in a purely physical way, it was Faith he loved and wanted to be with, Faith who was with him now, living at his flat, sharing his bed, and his thoughts and his dreams. And she was nice, too . . . likeable . . . which made everything so much worse.

I have got, Kit told herself sternly, to stop thinking about those two. She thought of her trip to Scotland instead, and suddenly longed to be there. Perhaps she could make the journey earlier, now that Harriet had gone home. Perhaps she could change her tickets and travel to Cannoch Moor on Saturday night, instead of

Monday. She felt it was worth a try. Once away, right away, she would be able to sort herself out. Loving a man wasn't everything, there were other things in life . . . plenty of things. She switched her radio on.

An hour later she had passed through Cawnford and was driving along a stretch of country road with the Downs on her left-hand side. It was still only eight o'clock and couples were walking high up on Furzedown Tye, a dog's shrill barking cut the silence, the sun was low in the sky. A man in a yellow sweater was leaving the bridle path, his shadow moving before him, with a vital life of its own. Kit recognised both, she would have recognised Charles—for that was who it was—in silhouette, with her eyes tightly shut; there was more to recognition than simply seeing. She began to slow the car.

She did so almost without volition, almost against her will. The sensible thing would be to pass by, as though she hadn't seen him, but it was too late for that, for he had seen her; he was raising a yellow-clad arm. He was hurrying towards her, and she rolled the window down. 'Do you want a lift into Bewlis,' she asked, 'or are you out for a walk?'

Charles had seen the car before she halted; he had seen it from higher up, like a moving red bead, speeding round the bend, and he couldn't believe his eyes when he saw that he knew its driver; he had been going to thumb a lift. 'You must be the answer to my prayer, Kit! I'm due at the hospital in a quarter of an hour, and I've cut things too fine. I might still make it if I put on a hustle, but now that you've come . . .' he raised an expressive brow.

'Get in,' she smiled, and opened her passenger door.

'I've been getting rid of my cricks and frustrations, up there on the heights,' he said as he climbed in beside her, reaching for the belt and clunking it in, and folding up his legs.

'Walking on the Downs always irons me out,' Kit confessed, as his shoulder bumped hers. The scent of grasses and gorse and breeze clung to his hair and sweater, vying with the aura that was his alone. She felt her heart contract.

The car moved forward, and she found that having to concentrate on the road, and the heavier traffic as they neared Bewlis, had a steadying effect. She was a first-rate driver, and knew she was; she felt confident and at ease. It couldn't last, this shot in the arm of simple, quiet happiness, but while it was here, why not enjoy it? She began to tell Charles about her journey to Kent, and her altered holiday plans.

She pulled out to pass a Southdown bus, and its green sides filled his window. He transferred his gaze inwards and looked at Kit, sitting straight and alert in her seat. He looked at her slightly parted lips, at her denim skirt which had rucked, at her long, slim legs ending in sandals. Why on earth did women wear shoes designed to cripple them? 'How's the small daughter?' he asked, once the bus was left behind.

'Absolutely fine, thanks,' she smiled, but kept facing front. She knew she ought to ask about Faith, for getting blown up . . . or very nearly . . . was no small thing, and it was less than two weeks ago. But somehow or other she couldn't make the simple, polite enquiry. Anyway, there wasn't time, for here was the hospital. Charles was already undoing his belt, and telling her not to bother to drive inside; he would get out at the gates.

'You've had enough driving for one day, I'm sure,' he told her.

'A few more yards won't make very much difference!' How lovely to defy him, and sweep inside; he couldn't escape till she stopped.

She drew up to the right of the doors leading to Casualty. He could cut through to the lifts from here, so he certainly wouldn't be late . . . probably ten minutes to the good, allowing time to get into his coat and brush his hair down flat.

'Thank you, you saved my life!' The hand he had stretched out to depress the door catch didn't do so, it dropped back into his lap. Then it moved again, upwards and across; it turned her face to his. 'Enjoy the rest of your holiday North of the Border, Kit.' His breath fanned her lips, and his kiss, this time, was the brief affectionate kind—the kind that married couples exchange when meeting or parting in public. Even so it drew the soul from her body. She would never get over him, she was quite sure she never would . . . most likely, even in Scotland, he would be there beside her, walking over the hills.

CHAPTER TWELVE

BUT THE trip to Scotland was not to be, for next day it was plain to see that Dee had caught her grandmother's cold. Her nose ran, she was fretful, she had to be coaxed to eat. She didn't want to get out of her cot, but wouldn't lie down in it, just stood on her blankets with slack knees, looking at her mother with woebegone eyes . . . how could you let this be?

'I'm going to call the doctor,' said Kit, during the afternoon. Peg was inclined to pooh-pooh the idea.

'You're fussing far too much. Joe had colds at that age, but he never took any harm. Dee will be better in a day or two. But I suppose you know best,' she said lamely, watching Kit go to the phone.

Dr Melksham, a parent himself, made no bones about calling. He arrived at Hilldown just before his evening surgery. Taking the thermometer away from Dee's armpit, he held it up to the light. 'Yes, as I thought . . . she's mildly pyrexic, but I don't think you need to worry. I'll write her up for some drops that will ease her nasal obstruction. What age is she now . . . fourteen months? My word, how time flies, Mrs Tennant! It seems only yesterday I was diagnosing your pregnancy. Now, if she should develop a cough, call me again. Good day to you.' He went off, banging the door.

Neither Dee nor Kit got very much rest that night. Dee slept a little, but had crying spells, and wouldn't be comforted. Towards morning she was coughing and her temperature was higher. When she breathed in there was harshness; it was this that alarmed Kit the most. She must get Dr Melksham at once . . . at once! The sound of the baby's cough tore at her own throat, and quickly she picked up the phone.

It was early, there was no one at the surgery, and she got the answering service. It gave her another number to ring, but that would probably mean . . . would most likely mean that a doctor she didn't know would arrive at the house. All GPs were used to children's ailments, so whoever came out on the call would be efficient, she didn't doubt that, but she wanted someone she knew. She wanted a specialist in children's complaints, she wanted the best for Dee. She thought of Hugh and dialled his number . . . medical etiquette, the fact that a consultant only saw a patient after a GP's referral, meant nothing to her. Hugh was a friend and he'd come.

It was seven-fifteen . . . would he be up? His phone was ringing now, she could hear it, hear the burring tone. Suppose he was asleep? Suppose he'd been up all night on a case, suppose he wasn't there? 'Hugh MacBride.' In the end his reply burst like a bomb on her ear.

'Hugh, thank goodness! Hugh, it's Katherine.'

There was a long pause, then: 'Yes?' he said, and nothing else at all.

'Hugh, can you help me . . . please, can you help me? Dee isn't well. She had what I thought was a cold yesterday, and I called in my doctor. He prescribed drops, and I've been instilling them, but she's not had a very good night. This morning she's coughing, there's inspiratory stridor, her temp is 39C. I tried to ring the surgery, but got the answering service. I didn't want a doctor from the pool. I thought . . . Hugh, can you come?'

There was no answer. Kit gripped the phone, thinking her head would burst. 'Are you there . . . Hugh, did you hear, are you there?'

'Yes, I'll come right away,' was his even reply, then she heard his receiver go down.

'What's going on? Is Dee worse?' Peg, in her tenth

week of pregnancy, didn't have good early mornings herself; she sat on the stairs whey-faced.

'She's having breathing difficulties.' Kit, with Dee rolled in a blanket, was walking up and down, soothing the child, trying to stop her coughing.

'Oh, no, Kit . . . oh, poor little mite! Who were you ringing?'

'Hugh.'

'Well, thank goodness you had that much sense.' Peg went upstairs to get dressed, and to tell Bob, and to keep Joe out of the way.

It was exactly eight o'clock when Hugh's silver Jaguar drew to a halt outside the gate. Kit felt she couldn't wait for him to get out and come into the house. 'I've left the door open,' she called from the window, as she stood with Dee in her arms.

'Well now, Delia, what's this I've been hearing about you?' He took the baby from her and talked to her quietly. Distressed though she was, Dee knew him, and by the time she was back in Kit's arms he had her confidence, even her trust, which was what he'd been aiming for. He took out his stethoscope, but before using it he watched Dee's breathing for depth and regularity and expansion of the chest wall. Kit positioned her so that he could so; she had done this often before, with other toddlers, when she had nursed at St Margaret's, when Hugh had been in charge. But now . . . now it was entirely different; she might be holding Dee with expertise and efficiency, but she held her as a mother. It was a mother's arms that supported the baby, a mother's eyes that watched Hugh's face. A mother's anxiety, not a nurse's interest, awaited the result of his examination, which didn't take very long.

Dee didn't mind the warmed stethoscope being placed on her front and back, but she didn't like her mouth being opened, while Hugh looked down her throat. He saw what he expected—a thick, viscous coating over her trachea and larynx. He closed is bag and stood up.

'I must admit her, Katherine. She has a virus infection, producing laryngo-tracheitis . . . not serious in an adult, but in a child of her age . . . well, we'll have her in, be on the safe side. I'll telephone the hospital from here, if I may, tell them what to expect. I'll take her in the car . . . both of you, of course,' he added, seeing Kit's face. 'You can stay in with her, you know, as a resident parent, for as long as it takes . . . if you want to, that is.'

'Yes, I do, I want to be with her.'

'Good—well, while I'm talking to Sister, get Delia ready, roll her in an eiderdown or duvet, and get a bag packed for yourself.' He closed the door firmly when he went out to telephone.

Peg and Bob came down to see them off, and then it was into the car, and being driven through the morning traffic to Cawnford and St Margaret's hospital. The big E-shaped building, set back from the road, was familiar to Kit, and she knew the fine reputation it had earned. The lift ticked them up to the third floor. Hugh chatted to the liftman about the proposed Channel tunnel link; all Kit could concentrate on was Dee's breathing. Oh, hurry, hurry . . . Vallance Ward at last, the corridor, the ward doors . . . and Sister coming to greet them, showing them to a cubicle away from the other cots.

Dee was to be nursed in a steam tent—different from an oxygen tent in that it didn't completely enclose her, merely the head of the cot. She was placed under the canopied end, and laid against piled pillows. Air was released under pressure through a container of water, creating a vapour which circled round her head.

'The steam will stop her secretions from drying, help her get rid of them, making it easier for her to breathe,' the young Sister explained.

'I think Mrs Tennant knows that, Sister.' Hugh was taking a swab from Dee's throat. 'She nursed at St

Margaret's on Parker Ward two years ago, you'll find her very useful.' He handed the specimen jar to Sister, who was so surprised at his words that she nearly dropped it.

'*Well*,' she said, 'I can do with more help on this ward.'

'Pending the lab's findings I'd like the patient put on a course of benzyl-penicillin and gentamycin.' Hugh stroked his beard, as he straightened up from the cot.

He and Sister went out to the office, while Kit remained with Dee, touching her head through the bars and letting her know that she was near. But when Hugh had gone Sister came back and showed her where she would sleep—in a small dormitory with three other mothers, halfway along the corridor. There was every facility, for St Margaret's was one of the newer hospitals. There was even a small sitting-room, with an alcove kitchen, where mothers could make themselves snack meals.

Kit was given a tabard overall to wear in the ward. She was also given breakfast, which she ate determinedly. Without food she couldn't function, and function she must. Between breakfast and lunch she was with Dee constantly, charting her observations, changing her bedding which soon became damp from the steam in the tent, giving her sips of water, talking quietly to her, singing softly, and praying; she never ceased doing that. I'll never ask for anything else, if only Dee gets well . . . I'll never even *want* for anything else if I can have her back safe and strong, she thought.

She ate her lunch with the three other mothers, who had also been keeping vigil by their children's cots. A staff nurse sat with Dee. The short time away from the ward . . . she had had to be pushed through the doors . . . gave her the respite she needed, and the opportunity to listen to the others' worries about their children. It helped to talk, it didn't lessen nor take away the fear, but it bound the three young women together in a kind of desperate friendship. They felt they had known one another for years.

Dee's condition remained much the same all day, but towards evening her temperature had risen to 40C, and Hugh came to see her again. Kit was asked to leave the ward while he examined her child. She found this very hard to bear, but had to bite on the fact that although she was helping to nurse Dee, she was first and foremost her mother, and mothers were seldom, if ever, present when doctors and staff conferred. But what were they saying, deciding, discussing? She knew that if Dee's throat didn't soon clear, a tracheostomy would have to be performed. The equipment was on her locker, it could be life-saving, Kit knew. She must be sensible and think of Dee solely as a patient, which was not only difficult, but quite impossible.

The two night nurses came on duty, neither of whom Kit knew. One was a Learner, round and jolly, the other a staff nurse with grey hair cut in a helmet fringe. It was she who asked Kit if she would like a camp-bed put up beside Dee's cot. 'You may feel you want to be near her all night.' She didn't say more than that, but it was plain that Sister's hand-over report had stressed the seriousness of Dee's condition. A bed was brought into the ward.

It was a long night, easily the longest Kit had ever spent. Her bed was used only for sitting on, for she couldn't lie down and relax. There was still so much to be done for Dee, and she wanted to do it herself. If only her temperature would start to go down, if only her cough would loosen, her breathing ease . . . if only Dee could rest!

It was five-thirty, and the Learner nurse was squeezing into the cubicle and asking Kit if she would like some tea, when Dee began to show the first obvious signs of change. It was her temperature . . . two points down.

Kit couldn't believe it at first. Staff Nurse was summoned, who sent for the registrar, Robert Farthingdale: 'We've been hoping for this.' He bent over the cot; the baby was asleep, her mouth was open, but there was no harsh, shrill sound when she breathed, and although she coughed, it was easily, and to good productive effect. 'We'll see a steady improvement, now,' Dr Farthingdale smiled at Kit. 'The steam therapy and antibiotic, not to mention the nursing, have done the trick. In another week she'll be well.'

Dee got steadily stronger as each day passed. Peg and Bob came to see her; they had to come separately; Joe being under twelve years old wasn't allowed to visit —this was a very strict St Margaret's rule. The phone in the resident parents' sitting-room was always ringing for Kit. Harriet rang from Kent every day, sometimes twice a day. She had been distraught when she heard that Dee was ill. 'To think I gave that germ to her! Kit, if anything had happened, if she'd died, what would I have done . . . how could I have borne it?' How could *I* have borne it, thought Kit, what would *I* have done? But she found room in her heart to comfort Harriet. Her parents rang from Scotland. They too were very upset. 'We'll be coming down to see you, darling, once Dee is discharged,' they said. There were get-well cards from several friends. Joe had made his own, and put three big kisses on the front.

On Thursday, the day before Dee's discharge, Sister came to tell Kit that there was a visitor for her and the baby. 'A Mr Niall,' she said. Kit was in the play-area, drawing a cat for Dee. There was a fair amount of noise going on, four children with the play-leader were having a game of Snakes and Ladders, with a good deal of squabbling. It isn't Charles's scene, flashed through her mind, seconds before he came in, carefully closing the sound proof door which led through from the ward. But when she saw him, as her eyes took him in, as she saw him crossing the carpet, stepping over scattered toys, she felt a wash of emotion so strong that she couldn't contain it. She battled but lost the fight. She hadn't shed a tear since Dee's illness, she hadn't even been able to weep relieving tears when she started to get well. But now . . . now she couldn't stop. She covered her face with her hands, just as Charles reached her and folded her into his arms.

'Oh, Kit darling—Kit darling!' She heard his murmured words. She felt his shirt against her face, his hand at the back of her head. He stroked her hair, he let her cry, and he swallowed against the stiffness in his own throat . . . and he told her she was brave.

She felt better afterwards. 'It's natural reaction,' said Charles as she blew her nose. 'You've had a stressful time, it must have been hell. I heard about it from Peg. I saw her last evening, in the High Street, walking along with Joe.'

They sat down, and he looked at Dee in her yellow dungarees. 'You've had a rough time, little Delilah.' He relinquished Kit's hand, and kneeling on the floor with the baby, he completed the sketch of the cat, crayoning in a bow around its tail. 'When was she actually admitted?' he asked, as Kit picked her up.

'Last Saturday. I rang Hugh direct—cut a few corners, I'm afraid. All I hope is he's been able to make things right with my own doctor—ethics being what they are!' She managed a watery smile.

'I'm sure he will.' Charles's legs were crossed, one hand lay on his knee, and she stared at it.

'Is Faith OK?' she asked.

'Yes, she's at her Newquay place. I had my parents at the flat as well, you know, we were tucked up for space. Still, there it was . . . desperate stiuations called for desperate measures.' He broke off as Hugh MacBride came in, looking round for Kit. Two of the children shrieked, '*Hello*!' and made a dive for him.

Charles got up and so did Kit; Hugh was politely stiff. 'It's not often we see you at St Margaret's, Charles. Would you like to see over the place?'

'Another time, perhaps,' Charles replied, equally stiffly. 'It was Kit and the baby I came to see, and having accomplished that, I think I'd better be getting back to my own territory.'

'I'll come with you, down to the entrance,' Kit wanted more time with him, but the door opened and Sister came in. She held out her arms for the baby.

'You're wanted on the telephone, in the sitting-room, Mrs Tennant. It's Mrs Tennant senior.'

Well, it *would* be, of course! Trust Harriet to ring at the wrong moment. Kit could hardly ask Charles to wait, especially as he was now showing signs of wanting to get away. So off she went, throwing 'goodbyes' and 'thank you's' over her shoulder. In his role of host, Hugh escorted Charles to the lifts.

Hugh had said he would drive Kit and Dee home next day, but shortly before they were due to leave he rang through to the ward to say that he been delayed. 'I think it would be as well to make other arrangements, Katherine. I don't know how long I'm likely to be, and . . .'

'Oh, Hugh, don't worry,' Kit was quick to say, 'I know Bob will fetch us. Please don't worry, I'm just very grateful for all you've done for me.'

'For Delia, surely.'

'It's much the same thing,' she said with a nervous laugh, feeling corrected and firmly set back into place.

The weather was perfect over the next few days. Kit and Dee, with Peg and Joe, spent most of the time in the garden. Dee's face filled out, her dimples reappeared, her skin turned apricot-peach, just like her mother's. 'I did just wonder,' said Peg one afternoon, 'if, during your time at St Margaret's, you might have changed your mind . . . over Hugh, I mean . . . discovered that . . .'

'Sorry, no.' Kit's voice was firm.

'Bob says you're in love with Charles Niall.' Peg's half-query dropped like the plop of a stone into a pool. Kit's first thought was to laugh and say, 'Rubbish!' but instead she told the truth.

'Bob's right—I am. And much good will it do me, but don't let it worry you. I shan't be eating my heart out for him. I'm going to apply for a transfer to another ward, where I shan't see him. I'm not the type to pine!'

'*He*'s not the type to settle down to family life,' said Peg. 'Look, Kit, for what it's worth, I think I should tell you something. I wasn't going to mention it, not unless I had to. It was something Harriet told me when she was here on holiday. We were talking about Tim . . . well, that was natural enough. She said she'd met a friend of his recently, someone called Peter Haines. The name rang a bell, and I remembered that you and Tim had gone to his wedding.'

'That was when I first . . . met Charles, on a collision course!' said Kit lightly, feeling her heart beating uncomfortably hard. What was Peg leading up to, what was she going to say?

'Harriet told this Haines man that you were nursing at the Bewlis General, and he asked if you knew a chap called Niall, who he thought had obtained a post there. Apparently, Charles was at one time engaged to a girl who was bosom friends with Peter's wife.'

'Hence the invitation to the wedding, obviously.' Kit's mouth was paper-dry.

'At the time of the wedding they were only a few weeks off their own. The girl was a widow, by the way, the child was about two years old. Charles jilted her, at the last minute, called the wedding off. They had a house, furnished, everything was ready, and he just backed out. Now, before you say that was three years ago, and nothing to do with you, think, Kit . . . just *think* about it.'

'What happened to the girl?' asked Kit.

'She went abroad, so Peter Haines said, her people lived in Canada. Peter's wife was very cut up about it all.'

'She would be, I suppose. And I also suppose that Harriet knew you'd be bound to tell me about this some time. She likes to run down my friends. If she had her way she'd have Dee and me living back at Alverstone, and she'd run our lives for us, and keep everyone else away.'

'I know she's possessive,' said Peg quietly, 'but even counting that, think carefully about what she said—I don't want to see you hurt.'

'I've just told you I shan't be seeing Charles any more than I can help, and then only professionally.' Kit retreated behind her book, but the print conveyed nothing to her. All she saw on the page was Charles. Could he have behaved like that? He might have loved the girl to distraction, but perhaps, as time went on, the thought of taking on her child as well had proved too much. But to do it like that, so cruelly, so suddenly, so near their wedding day. Harriet must have got it wrong, or twisted the truth deliberately. On the other hand, it could be true. Everything Charles had said . . . and once in public . . . led one to think that he didn't want encumbrances. And what could be a bigger encumbrance, a bigger little millstone round one's neck, than someone else's child? Charles had the kind of relationship he wanted, Faith suited him perfectly. And anyway, why am I worrying myself about it like this? she thought. I've made up my mind to avoid him, haven't I? She had, and that was why it was so inexplicable to her, as well as to Peg, that when Charles rang up next evening and invited her out to dinner, she said, 'Yes' without a second's thought.

'You're mad!' Peg exploded.

'I know, but I'm still going.'

'He's at a loose end, Faith's still away.'

'I know, but I'm still going!' Kit sobered suddenly. 'Look, Peg, I'm going for *fun*. It's my holiday, remember, and it's not been exactly riotous, so far. The first week Harriet was here, and the week after that I was incarcerated in a children's hospital, worried out of my mind. Tomorrow night I'm dressing up and going out on a date . . . a date with Charles, for better or worse. I can take care of myself, and of my feelings, so stop going on and on!'

'I got the distinct impression,' said Charles over dinner the following night, 'that your cousin wasn't all that thrilled about you coming out. There wasn't a babysitting problem, was there?'

'Oh no, nothing like that.' Kit smiled at him; on her second glass of wine she was feeling . . . comfortable. Charles had brought her to the Downs Hotel, at the western end of the town. It stood at the foot of Carle Beacon and commanded arresting views. They were in the Lansdown Restaurant with its domed glass ceiling. Dusk was falling, and the lights had been switched on.

'Perhaps,' he finished his whitebait, and buttered the last of his roll, 'perhaps Peg wishes your dinner dates were confined to Hugh MacBride.'

'Perhaps she does.' Kit retrieved her napkin, which had fallen on to the carpet.

'Are you going to marry him?' His face, when she straightened, was very close to hers.

'I think you've asked me that before.'

'But I didn't get a straight answer.'

'Hugh has never asked me to marry him,' she took a calming breath, 'not in actual words, I mean. He just brought the subject up—the subject of marriage and Dee having a father—in a testing kind of way. I didn't want him to ask me, because I didn't want to have to say no. He's been good to me, and to Dee . . . It was very difficult.'

'He always seemed to be around, you were always in his company,' Charles observed.

'Not so much as all that,' Kit said sharply. 'I didn't string him along, if that's what you mean. Hugh knew from the start that I didn't intend to remarry.'

'Some men,' Charles leaned back while the waiter removed their plates, 'would see that as a challenge.'

'I was never unfair to him!' Kit protested.

'I'm sure you weren't, he touched her arm, 'you're not that kind of girl.'

Their main course was set in front of them, the vegetables and sauces served. The waiter moved to top up Kit's glass, but she stopped him, shaking her head. Her comfortable feeling of state and mind was slipping away like clothes, leaving her so aware of the man beside her on the banquette that she couldn't or didn't want to eat. The mirrored pillar opposite reflected their images —showed a titian-haired girl in a black dress, with the neckline cut in a vee, showed her partner sitting tall beside her, svelte in a dinner jacket, his face in profile as he turned his head to her. 'Remember the first time we met, at that fateful wedding?' he asked.

'I remember it perfectly.'

'I nearly married the girl I was with that day.'

Kit found herself holding her breath. He was going to tell her about it; he must be, or he wouldn't have brought the subject up. She felt like asking, 'What happened, did you jilt her?' but a glance at his face—the one beside her, not the one in the mirror—made her hold her tongue.

'Madeleine was a widow, her baby was Dee's age when we met. She was a secretary at the Royal, the hospital in Berkshire, where I held a junior registrar's post. I fell in love with her on sight,' Charles said simply, 'I grew to love her child. We all three seemed to knit together, to be a family. There were snags, of course . . . my parents were against us, especially my father, who went on about me saddling myself with a ready-made family. He admitted that Madeleine was a good mother, but said that her prime concern was to provide herself with a meal ticket and her child with a father. I didn't believe him, or didn't choose to, but he turned out to be right.

'Madeleine knew, when we went to the Haines' wedding, that an old boyfriend of hers would be there, someone she'd known before she was married. He was over from Canada. He too was a friend of the bride's, a very prosperous one, something to do with forestry; Madeleine was very impressed. The upshot of this old-flame meeting was that she swapped me for him three weeks later—just walked out, carrying Claire. A month after that she was married and going out to Montreal. Her parents had been there some years, which I suppose was an added attraction.'

'How awful!' Kit sympathised, while her thoughts rioted. Charles hadn't let the girl down, after all; his was the true version of the whole affair, she knew that instinctively. No man would ever say he'd been jilted if the reverse was the case. And apart from that, aside from that, Charles wouldn't let anyone down, not without very good reason, and never cruelly.

'It was grim at the time, I admit,' he said, laying down his fork. 'Everything reminded me of Madeleine, and if ever I met a child of Claire's age, I wanted to cut and run. Selling the house, clearing it out, was a very painful experience, certainly not helped by my father's I-told-you-so's.'

'Oh dear . . . parents!' Kit thought of Harriet. 'Still,' she said, 'you stuck it out, you didn't change your job.'

'Registrars' jobs don't grow on trees. I carried on till I came here. End of case history!' Charles smiled at her, then looked down at her plate. 'You've not eaten very much, have you? Would you like something else?'

'Oh no, thanks,' she shook her head, 'the first course filled me up.'

'Shall we settle for coffee—have it out on the patio? Then, just for a change, you can tell me a little about yourself.'

'All right, if you like.'

He summoned the waiter. Kit went to get her wrap—a white mohair stole, a foil for her dress, an enhancement of her hair which looked darker in the dimmer lights out on the patio. Charles watched her as she came towards him. The waiter pulled up a table in front of a long cushioned seat, then left them together to enjoy their coffee in welcome solitude.

The town lay below them—a tapestry of lights, spreading away to the south. They could pick out landmarks, see the hospital with its rearing tower block. The straight horizon in the far distance they knew was the English Channel; they could smell the Downs and the salty tang of the sea. 'It's worth coming out for.' Charles cleared his throat.

Kit agreed that it was. She supposed he had brought Faith here many times, and although, just at the moment, Faith was the very last person she wanted to talk about, she asked about her, asked when she'd be coming back.

'She'll be back to pack up, next week, I think. She's decided to sell the remainder of her shop lease to the chap who's running it now. She wants to live in Newquay, she has several friends down there.'

Kit's coffee flopped and burnt her lip; for a second she couldn't speak. 'It won't be so easy for you to meet, once she's down there for good,' she managed to say, and was proud of her nonchalant voice.

'If we wanted to meet, it's no great distance,' Charles pointed out.

'No, I suppose it's not.'

'It so happens we don't.' She saw his arm move as he set his coffee cup down.

'I'm sorry, I didn't mean to be . . . I didn't mean to be nosey.' And now she was flustered, while something in her rejoiced.

'You're not nosey at all.' He smiled at her then, and no one in the world smiled quite like Charles Niall; Kit felt her insides knot. 'Faith's and my relationship,' he went on, 'wasn't the permanent kind. We both knew that, there were no promises, and it petered to an end during our Cornish holiday in June. Our last date was the Centenary Ball; I'd promised to take her to that weeks before, and I needed a partner, so you could say she helped me out . . . as I helped her, or tried to, when her premises were wrecked.'

'Oh, I see. Oh, well . . . I liked Faith.' Kit ducked her head. She was afraid to look at Charles in case he read her expression aright. He didn't love Faith . . . he didn't love Faith! Just at that moment, the relief she felt must be printed across her face.

'But talking of that Centenary Dance,' Charles shifted beside her, 'I would like to apologise for my crass statement about young widows. It wasn't a bitter allusion to my past . . . I can't make that the excuse. I said it deliberately for you to hear. I was jealous of MacBride.'

'Jealous of Hugh? But . . .' She got no farther, for a dozen or so diners filed out on to the patio, filling the air with noise and cigar smoke and after-dinner jokes.

'Let's go down into the gardens, we can't hear ourselves speak up here.' Charles took Kit's arm and they went down the flight of steps to the sunken gardens —an attractive feature of the hotel. 'Why are you so determined not to marry again?' he asked as they halted by the ornamental pond. 'Were you so happy with your husband that you feel nothing will ever match that, or were you,' he took her hand, and held it tightly in his, 'were you, perhaps, not so happy, and are afraid to try again?'

She didn't pull away from him, but he felt the jerk she gave. 'I loved Tim,' she said quietly, 'and I know he loved me, but we were two different people, and it was . . . sometimes difficult.'

She said nothing else, she didn't have to; he filled in the missing pieces. She had been unhappy, that was obvious, she had had a chequered life with a weak man who had given her nothing at all. 'You know, don't you,' he said softly out of the silence that followed, 'that I'm completely and absolutely under your spell? You've bewitched me.' He kissed her before she could speak. 'And that means I love you, dearly love you,' he kissed her again. 'The first spark flared upwards when you told me off at that wedding! Then when you came to the General, and I saw you in the corridor, tripping along, pushing that trolley, I thought my world had caved in. You see,' he held her face between his hands, and smiled at her, 'I didn't want to love you, that was the last thing I wanted. It was too much, too laughable, too deadly serious—to fall in love with a widow with a baby, all over again. History was repeating itself, and so much more painfully. You already had a handsome suitor in the shape of Hugh MacBride, all ready to whisk you off . . . you and your child.'

'I like Hugh, but love is different,' Kit told him softly.

'Do you feel it for me?' His face was very close to hers, less than an inch away.

'I've loved you since the day of the Show,' was all she managed to say before their lips met, and pressured, and said things that words could not, generating a tide of feeling that filled all the lonely places in each of them. It was hard to draw apart.

'Will you marry me, darling? Will you take a chance? I'll make you happy, I swear. I want you for my wife, and

Dee for my daughter . . . I want us together in marriage.' Charles wasn't sure, even now, that she'd have him. Supposing she turned him down, supposing she stuck to her vow about never marrying again.

'Charles, are you sure . . . a readymade family? Charles, are you sure?' She tried to see his face in the dark, she traced it with her fingers.

He crushed her to him. 'I've never been more sure. I've never in my life loved anyone so much. I want you with me for always . . . you and Dee.'

'I want that too, so the answer is yes . . . yes, Charles, I'll marry you.'

'My sweet enchantress . . . my dearest one!' He brought his head down to hers. And this time their kiss was a promise, unhurried, then quickening to fire, to a flare of passion that spoke of his longing for her, and hers for him, and the love that would bind them, through all the years to come.

They thought their news would surprise everyone, but that wasn't really the case. Charles's father, not unnaturally, said that his son must have a penchant for widows with babies, but he wished them luck all the same.

Bob was delighted, and his enthusiasm conveyed itself to Peg, who said she had always thought Charles was gorgeous, but a little out of reach.

And Harriet—well, Harriet needed to be reassured. Kit took Charles to see her a fortnight before their wedding. The perhaps not too surprising thing was that she fell for him on sight. 'But, Kit dear, he's so strong and big, yet so gentle underneath. He'll be a wonderful father to Dee, and he'll let me come and see her . . . he said so, when you're married, I mean; he says I can come to stay.'

Kit was going to sell Hilldown when Peg and Bob moved out. Charles and she were buying a Victorian house a little way down the road, the house with the monkey-puzzle tree in the front garden. The family who lived there were moving to Kingston-on-Thames.

But it wasn't until their wedding day on the fourteenth of October that Harriet confessed to her sin of trying to blacken Charles's name. 'I did it for your protection, dear. I mean, I wasn't to know how nice he was, and how suitable—I had no idea at all. I thought he might be like the other doctor with a beard.'

'Hugh was a dear,' said Kit stoutly. And exactly a year later someone else plainly thought so too—in the shape of Sister Clive. When Hugh landed a new consultancy post in Edinburgh, Sister Clive went with him as his wife, and a year after that she bore him twin daughters, with the minimum of fuss.

Charles made the point that twins must be the fashionable thing at the moment, for upstairs in the nursery lay his own son and daughter, six months old—a pigeon pair; a brother and sister for Dee.

Dee, at three and a half, was tall and leggy, and full of fun. She had a swing in the garden, and a sandpit like Joe's, and she dearly loved her father . . . very nearly as much as her mother, who sometimes wondered what she had done to deserve so much happiness.

Tell
Me
No
Lies
ELIZABETH
LOWELL